A BRUNCH WITH DEATH

COMPASS COVE COZY MYSTERY BOOK 2

MARA WEBB

CHAPTER 1

"*L*isten, cat, you either start helping and assist me with this spell, or I'm sending you to the shelter for annoying talking animals."

"Me-*owch*," Hermes responded cattily. "May I remind you that I'm not a cat? I'm a *familiar*. I used to be a wizard once you know, though that was a long time ago. I was the 'Fantastic Hermes!' Soothsayer to the wealthy, medic-extraordinaire to the poor. A true saint of my time! You know, a local princess once took fancy with me and—"

"I'm going to stop you right there," I said, putting a hand in the air to pull the brakes before Hermes started another one of his rambling stories. "Are you going to help me with this spell or not?"

"I *am*, what's the big deal? I've been helping you for like the last hour! I'm one of the best familiars in town I'll have you know!"

'Helping' was a choice word, because in the last hour that Hermes had been in this room while I was preparing my spell, he had been asleep for most of the time, and when he was awake, he'd mostly just been criticizing my 'wand posture' and Latin pronunciation.

"Maybe prove it then, eh?" I said, scratching my knuckles over the top of his head in a loveable but rough way. "Now where were we? Ah yes, the top of this page. *Incanto Alorum—*"

1

"Incanto," Hermes interrupted, pronouncing the word the exact same way that I had.

"What?" I asked.

"It's Incanto, not *Incanto*. You're saying the 'cant' part like it rhymes with *plant*, but you need to say 'cant' so it rhymes with *shan't*." He then paused and put on an awful English accent as if to demonstrate. "Thomas shan't have any scones for tea if he carries on being a naughty boy!" He blinked and looked at me. "Hopefully that clears it up."

"Clear as muck," I said. "Does the pronunciation matter all that much? If I'm saying the words in the right order and my intent is clear in my mind, then who cares if my words are tone perfect? Magic isn't a tonal language. Right?" I asked after a pause of panic. I'd spent a few weeks trying to learn Mandarin one bored summer and given up after my brain nearly melted out my ears.

"There are actually two schools of thought on that matter," Hermes said, straightening his spine out and lifting his head as he got ready to open another long window of one-sided chatter. "The first group thinks it *does* matter, and I just so happen to belong to that group. The second group believes it doesn't matter. Now it's *true*, most of the time a spell *will* work perfectly well even if your pronunciation is off, but you just have to ask my friend Jimmy the Sock what happens if you don't pay *any* attention to pronunciation. The year was 1852 and—"

"What are you even talking about?!" I asked. "Who is Jimmy the Sock, and what happened to him?" I just desperately wanted to get the point of this story out of Hermes as quickly as possible so I could go back to my job at hand—finishing this spell.

"Jimmy was a regular farm boy, but he had magic in him, so a friend of mine took him under his wing and Jimmy became his apprentice. Jimmy was a brilliant young magician, but he paid no attention to his magical pronunciation when speaking incantations. He got away with it for a while mind, but one fateful day in the heatwave of '52, Jimmy tried a small spell to bring in a bit of rain for the crops. Well he didn't drop the 'oo' sound in the word *pluvia*—which is, of course, Latin for *rain*—and well we can all guess what happened next."

Hermes' story apparently ended there, because he nodded at me smugly and shifted his weight left and right slightly, seemingly satisfied with that mystifying ending.

I stared at him wide-eyed, shaking my head as though to dig the resolution up. "So, what happened? Why did I have to be burdened with the one familiar that is a walking clickbait article?"

"Well, isn't it obvious? He turned himself into a sock. Completely irreversible. He's still a sock to this day. In a local museum now of course; I go and visit him sometimes and talk. That guy can really tell a good yarn."

"Did you seriously make me sit through all that just to get to that punch line?" I sighed.

Hermes looked confused for a second. "Punch line? What do you— oh, yarn! Ha!" he said, laughing at his own accidental pun. "Oh, I'm a comedy genius! I didn't even realize!"

"Why did he turn into a sock though?" I asked. "Just because he pronounced a word wrong?"

"Huh?" Hermes said, snapping out from some brief trance. "Oh, well, no one actually knows what happened. We're just guessing, but his pronunciation *was* sloppy, so it's the most likely culprit."

I stared at Hermes for a moment, resisting the urge to grind my teeth. As usual it turned out his story didn't really have a point, and he had just been wasting my time. "...Right. Well, I'm going to keep on reading this spell, and you're going to sit there quietly. Okay?"

"Fine," he said, rolling his eyes dramatically. "But you need to hold your wand a bit more limply, your wand posture is all—" I shot Hermes a look that could boil water, and he zipped his mouth shut. "But you know what, it looks pretty good from here. Keep at it, sister!"

The spell I was trying to do was a fairly simple one by all accounts, all I was trying to do was to conjure a magical clock. Magic worked in different ways, depending upon how you did it. The first time I'd really seen magic in Compass Cove was when I met my sister Zelda.

Zelda magicked up a bowl of sugar cubes, and upon asking her where they'd come from, she'd given a simple answer—the kitchen ten feet behind her. When a witch conjured an item, she could either summon it from the real world, effectively teleporting the item into her hand, or she could actually *make* it. This second option of actually making an item from scratch took significantly more magic, so most of the time a witch would just go with the teleport option.

Why was I trying to conjure up a magical clock? It was one of the tests I'd been given, an entrance exam given to me after I'd applied to go to magical school. Apparently, it wasn't entirely uncommon for some witches to not get their powers until later in life, and a witch could apply to go to magic school at any age once she'd learned about her powers, *but* she had to demonstrate basic aptitude first and demonstrate some minor powers.

The school I had applied to had provided a short pamphlet which contained various magical tests, the last of which was this one: conjure a magical clock so the school could determine my skill level. The pamphlet featured a three-page spell which I had to read through, while performing basic gestures with my wand. I was allowed a familiar to assist me if I already had one, and unfortunately for me I did.

"I just don't know why you're stressing out about this so much," Hermes said after staying quiet for a record-breaking forty seconds, "It's just a magic clock. You've got this! You're a Prismatic Witch after all. This sort of thing is a walk in the park for someone like you!"

"I'm still allowed to feel nervous. This is a big deal for me, and I don't want to mess it up."

Since moving to Compass Cove and discovering I was a witch I'd had to visit my cousin Sabrina's magic shop to get a wand for myself. Apparently most witches fit into one of the five main types: Kitchen, Cosmic, Divination, Sea, or Green. Each different type specialized in various areas of magic. While trying to find a wand that was right for me, I was disappointed to find none of the wands would work. Sabrina quickly realized that I was an entirely different type of witch, a rare type that encompassed all the different archetypes—I was something they called a *Prismatic Witch*, someone gifted with a naturally heightened power. From what they tell me, apparently there are only a few known Prismatic Witches in the world, and now I was one of them.

"Yeah, but all good witches make a magic clock when they're first starting out, it's kind of like when kids have to make a wooden box in shop class. A rite of passage. The clock will be crumby, but it's yours for life," Hermes explained. "Stop sweating things, it doesn't have to be perfect. Just ticking is fine, doesn't even need to have any magical features."

"Well, I'd like it to have at least one magical feature," I said. "By the way, I can't help but feel that your constant interruptions are much worse for this spell than me mispronouncing some stupid Latin."

"Nah, we'll be fine. As long as you pick up exactly where you left it's not an issue. I once stopped an incantation one word before the end, forgot about, and I said it years later by accident. Constance was surprised when six oil barrels full of corn appeared in her lounge."

"Why on earth were you trying to conjure up six oil barrels full of corn in the—" I stopped myself. "No, you know what? I don't care. Stop distracting me and let me finish. I've got three paragraphs of Latin left to butcher, and I want to do it uninterrupted."

"Don't let me hold you back, girlfriend," Hermes said, fulfilling his insatiable need to always have the last word, no matter how helpful. Thankfully he was silent for the remainder of the short spell. I moved my wand through the air, following the posture prompts while reading the Latin. Wand movement prompts were sort of written directly over the words, squiggly lines that vaguely suggested what sort of shape you should draw in the air with the tip of your wand.

I wasn't sure if I was doing any of this right, but I just tried to hold the idea of a magical clock firmly in my mind; my cousin Sabrina and my sister Zelda told me that intention was one of the most important parts of magic.

As I got to the last few words of the spell, I wondered what kind of abilities my magical clock would have, if any at all. In the intro to the spell the pamphlet gave some examples of known abilities—some clocks could tell you the locations of loved ones, others could slow or speed up time—some could even stop time.

With the final words a strong magical surge swept through my wand, which began to vibrate vigorously in my hand. I saw beams of colored light moving under its surface. They burst forth from the tip with a powerful charge. A bright ball of white light burned in the air above the kitchen table, the light and the vibration ended, and I saw the end result on the tabletop.

"Wow, your clock looks like an owl!" Hermes said excitedly.

I stared at the end result of my spell in amazement, and when I saw the clock ruffle its feathers, move its wings, and blink its large yellow eyes slowly I realized it wasn't like an owl at all. "It... *is* an owl," I said in bewilderment.

"Wrong actually," the not-owl said in a high-strung voice that sounded feminine. "I'm an Olaphax."

"A what now?" I asked, looking at Hermes.

"Hey, don't look at me. I thought a Filofax was some relic of the eighties."

"An *Olaphax*," the strange talking bird corrected with another slow blink. "I guess you can be forgiven for calling me an owl. My kind gets that a lot."

"Uh... I was trying to conjure up a magical clock," I said slowly, wondering what on earth this thing was doing on my kitchen table.

"Yes..." the bird said, as if I stated the obvious.

"It's just... I can't help but notice you're not a clock. You're an owl."
And the award for observation of the year goes to...

"An Olaphax," the bird corrected.

"Right, sorry," I said.

"I told you," Hermes said smarmily. "You should have paid more attention to pronunciation, *and* wand posture. But no, you just stood there and berated your poor old familiar, thinking you know all that just because you think I'm full of it! Well now who's laughing, missy? You'll never get an owl to tell you the time!"

"It's 8:53 and 36 seconds," the not-owl said. "Pack an umbrella tomorrow because it's going to rain."

"Oh, oh, oh! I know what this thing is!" Hermes said excitedly. "It's a time owl!"

"A what now?" I asked.

"Time owl is a derogatory slur; no one uses that phrase anymore," the Olaphax said.

"What is a time owl?" I said to Hermes.

"Up until now I thought they were just made up, but I guess you *should* believe everything you read. You guys are like stewards of time, right?" he asked the magical bird.

"We time owls—I mean, *Olaphax,* are mere caretakers of time. We cannot control or change it, we simply observe it," the Olaphax said.

Staring at the magical owl I couldn't help but find myself entranced. She wasn't much bigger than a regular barn owl, but her entire body was covered with beautiful iridescent feathers that caught the light and changed color with each miniscule movement.

"You're beautiful," I gasped. "Do you have a name?"

"You may call me Phoebe. My real name would take several years to pronounce, and it would turn this town into a small crater."

"Right," I said with an unsure smile. "Well, I'm Zora, and this is my familiar, Hermes. I was trying to conjure up a magical clock, Phoebe, so I apologize. I'm not sure how you ended up here."

Phoebe blinked slowly. "Isn't it obvious? You conjured me. You must be a very powerful witch. Only a gifted magician can summon an Olaphax. It is a great blessing, a truly unique gift to possess."

"Are the time owls familiar with the concept of humility?" Hermes asked. I looked at him with a brow lifted. "What?!"

"Um, me thinks the pot is calling the kettle black a little," I said. "Be nice to Phoebe."

"So now you're taking sides with the time owl, unbelievable!" Hermes protested. I pushed him off the table and rolled my eyes.

"Sorry about that," I said to Phoebe. "Where did you come from then? How long will you be staying here?"

"Oh, I'm yours for life," Phoebe blinked. "You can think of me as another familiar, though I will be much more useful than a flea-ridden cat."

"It's good that the two of you are already getting on," I said sarcastically. "So, what can a time owl—sorry, I mean, what can an Olaphax do?"

"I have a wide range of abilities, chief of which are my abilities to tell the time and see into the present."

"Can't everybody see into the present? It's… happening right now," I said.

"A common mistake," Phoebe assured me. "Your perception of the present is roughly a second. My perception of the present is far greater. Approximately six of your hours."

"So you *can* see into the future?" I asked in a confused manner.

Phoebe just laughed. "I suppose to a human it would appear like that, but as someone who can actually see time I assure you; I can't see things that haven't already happened."

"Right."

"By the way your appointment with *Bitz and Bosch* is scheduled for tomorrow at 9am."

"Who now?" I asked. "When did I make an appointment?"

"You haven't made it yet," Phoebe said calmly.

"And you're telling me you can't see into the future?"

"That is correct," the owl blinked.

"Right, well. I think I'm going to make a cup of tea. Hermes! Hermes? Where are you?" I walked into the kitchen and went to turn the kettle on when I realized it was missing. I paused and looked at the empty spot, wondering where it could have possibly gone.

This wasn't the first time this had happened this week. Several objects had gone missing around my apartment over the last few days. At first, I thought it was Hermes messing with me, or maybe even my ghost Aunt Constance, but both denied the accusations vigorously.

"Zora, in here!" I heard Hermes shout from the corridor that led into my bedroom. "I caught one of them!"

"One of what?" I shouted back as I headed in his direction. What on earth was going on now?

CHAPTER 2

*a*s I came around the corner I saw Hermes on the floor, his front paws outstretched as he held on to something small and black.

"Is that a mouse?" I gasped. "Let go of it! Don't hurt it!"

"It's not a mouse!" Hermes snapped. "Get me a jar, pronto! I've been trying to catch one of these little buggers for days!"

I hurried back to the kitchen and came back a moment later with an empty glass jar. In a rare moment of joint coordination, we managed to capture the small black creature in the glass jar and sealed it. "It's a little person!" I said in amazement. Hermes looked less thrilled.

"It's a Poxy," Hermes said scornfully. "Horrible little buggers. The fact that they're in the apartment at all isn't good; in fact it's actually quite bad."

I crouched down basically all the way on the floor to look at the small ink-black person inside the jar. It was as if their body was made of black smoke, the edge of their silhouette wisping slightly with each animated movement—and believe me, there was a lot of movement.

The little Poxy hammered its fists against the glass walls of the jar, its mouth open wide as it shouted something at me. I couldn't make out the cries because they were muffled by the jar.

"It's like a little fairy," I said, noting the smokey black wings on its body. The Poxy was all black and didn't appear to have any clothes. The only identifiable features were its little white eyes—which looked angry—and two rows of sharp teeth in its mouth. "What's it trying to say?"

"It's trying to curse you," Hermes said with disinterest. "And it's probably trying to curse me too."

"Curse?" I asked.

"Yeah, they're not capable of anything truly terrible, but they can stick you with minor annoyances. Every time you run the kitchen sink the water from the faucet will hit a spoon. Your zipper never stays up, every time you eat popcorn you get a piece stuck in your teeth. Minor annoyances, that sort of thing. The Poxy folk thrive on things like that. Like I said, they're horrible."

"Why is it in the apartment?" I asked.

"Poxy are like magical vermin, they crop up from time to time. I had my suspicions some were here because things keep disappearing. They start with small things and then they work their way up until your entire house is gone."

"What?!"

"Relax, it takes a long time for them to get that brave. Mostly they just take hairpins and batteries."

"What do they do with them?"

Hermes shrugged. "I don't think anyone knows. They don't speak a lick of English and they disappear through little doorways, back into their wretched little realm. We can put down a few traps; that should keep them out."

"Wait, is that why the kettle is missing?" I asked, my mind flitting back to the kitchen. Hermes' eyes opened wide.

"They took a kettle?" he asked in alarm. "Okay, then maybe this is more serious than I realized. They shouldn't be taking things that large so quickly!" Hermes peered down into the jar and addressed the Poxy. "Where's the kettle, you little urchin!"

The Poxy responded to Hermes by giving him the one-finger salute, pulling an ugly face, and turning around and slapping its ass. "Wow, they really are charming," I said in dismay.

"Zora, this is worse than I realized," Hermes said. "If these little demons are already taking kettle-sized objects this infestation is worse than I assumed. You'll have to get a magical exterminator in."

"How do I do that?" I asked.

Hermes lifted his head and shouted, as though summoning a horse. "Phone book!"

Nothing happened for a moment, but suddenly a huge book flew out of a portal in the wall and caught me in the side of the head. I hit the opposite wall and dropped to the floor, the heavy book clutched in my hands. I brushed my hair off my face and scowled at Hermes. "Seriously? You couldn't have given me a heads-up?"

"It's not normally that fast!" he said defensively. "You can summon it whenever you need. It doesn't require any magic!"

I gathered up the book, the glass jar containing the Poxy, and went back into the apartment, placing both items on the living room table.

"What is that?" Phoebe said in disgust as she peered into the jar.

"A Poxy, apparently. Hermes will fill you in on the rest." I also crouched down and looked into the glass jar. "Tell me where my kettle is, or I'm going to feed you to this owl." Once again, the Poxy started dancing around obscenely in the jar, slapping its ass and letting me know what it thought of me.

"No way am I eating that thing!" Phoebe said. "It looks horrid!"

"How lost is this kettle?" I said to Hermes. "Like, already gone?"

"Probably not. They hide things in the house first; they need time to make a doorway to their little realm."

"Help me find the kettle. I'll make a cup of tea; we can have some cake while I look for an exterminator in the phonebook. Where do these Poxy creatures hide things usually?"

Hermes shrugged once again. "I don't know. Could be anywhere. Maybe in one of your boots?"

"You think a kettle could fit in one of my boots?" I said, looking down at my feet, which were currently warm in a pair of fuzzy pink slippers. "How big do you think my feet are?"

"Don't take this the wrong way, Zora, but your feet are freakishly large," Hermes said nonchalantly.

I stared at the cat for a moment, wondering why I let him stay around. "Let's just look for this kettle, yeah?"

"It's under the couch," Phoebe said, still standing on the same spot on the table as when she had first arrived. I turned and looked at her.

"How do you know?"

"You and the fleabag spend twenty minutes looking for it. Then he finds it under the couch."

"I can't believe this," I said.

"I know," Hermes chimed. "Who are you calling fleabag? No-ears!"

"Not that," I said. "The fact that *you* would actually be the one to find something." I looked under the couch, and sure enough there was the kettle, laying on its side. I picked it up and marched back to the glass jar on the table, holding the kettle triumphantly as I taunted the Poxy. "Not today, you little weirdo! Ha!"

In turn the Poxy grabbed its crotch and made a series of obscene gestures. I took the kettle back to the kitchen, boiled some water for the teapot, and grabbed a plate of caramel jam slices that I had made that morning. As I was carrying the items back to the kitchen table my younger sister Zelda came through the front door and dumped several bustling shopping bags onto the kitchen floor.

"It's bitter as anything out there!" she said, hanging up her scarf and coat. "How are you doing, sis?"

"Fine," I said. "I wasn't expecting you to drop around today. I just put the kettle on. Do you want some tea and cake?"

"You read my mind!" Zelda sang as she came over to the living room table. It wasn't until she had sat down that she noticed the owl and the Poxy in the glass jar. "Another busy morning for you then?" she asked with a note of amusement. "That owl is beautiful. Its feathers look like the forecourt of a gas station. Is it covered in oil? Is it a rescue? Can I help you clean it!?" Zelda, if you didn't notice, had a habit of letting her thoughts get away with her.

"The forecourt of a gas station?" Phoebe said with hearty offense. "And what about you? It looks like someone dragged you through a bush backwards!"

Zelda immediately blushed, apparently mortified to find the owl was sentient. "Oh gosh! I'm sorry, I didn't realize you were a familiar!"

"Familiar?" Phoebe threw her head back and laughed. "Don't put me in the same ranks as those circus act pets. I'm an Olaphax!"

"She's a time owl," Hermes said through his teeth. "And a rather annoying one at that."

A look of intrigue came over Zelda. "A time owl! I've always wanted to see one. I had a story as a child with a time owl in it. Is it true you can tell people when and how they die?"

"That's a common myth," Phoebe dismissed with a roll of her large yellow eyes.

"Yes, it appears that the time owl can only tell us the time and the weather forecast for the next twelve hours," Hermes said with a smirk. "She's basically a glorified smartphone."

"What does that make you? A footstool with a grating personality?" Phoebe quipped. Zelda and I had to stifle back our laughter.

"Don't take her side!" Hermes said.

"Sorry, but you have to laugh, Hermes. You dish it out, and now you've got someone to give it back to you in equal measure," I pointed out.

"Well, I don't like her. I think she should leave."

"You'll change your tune in two hours and fifteen minutes," Phoebe said cryptically. Hermes opened his mouth to respond, but just narrowed his eyes and glared at the time owl curiously.

"Why is it here?" Zelda asked.

"Oh, you know, tale as old as time. I was trying to conjure up a magical clock for my magic school application, and I somehow ended up with a talking rainbow owl."

"Olaphax," Phoebe corrected under her breath.

"Zora, I'm impressed," Zelda said. "This only goes to show your magic gifts are far beyond normal. Time owls are very powerful creatures, and once they appear to a witch, they're yours for life!"

"Why do I bother…" Phoebe said under her breath again, shaking her head in dismay.

"Will it affect my application?" I asked Zelda. "The task was to make a magical clock."

"I think it will only affect it positively," Zelda said. "This is a top marks type of result. I had to make a magic clock when I was younger; it was nowhere near as good as this. One hand only works on Wednesdays, and there's another hand that always tells me where Miriam Gooseman is."

"Who is Miriam Gooseman?" I asked.

"Just some girl that was in my class. We weren't even friends." Zelda turned her eyes on Phoebe again and looked enthralled. "Nothing like this. She's beautiful!"

"Oh stop," Phoebe said bashfully. After a moment she said, "Or carry on. I don't mind."

Zelda then noticed the Poxy in the glass jar. "Ugh, is that a Poxy?" She took a sip of her tea.

"Yeah, Hermes just caught it a few minutes ago." I put my hand on the phone book and pulled it towards me. "I'm going to call an exterminator. That little scoundrel had my kettle."

"Crikey, taking a kettle already? That's not a good sign. Yeah, I'd get an exterminator pronto. You don't want them to snatch the bakery from under your nose." Zelda grabbed a caramel jam slice and shoved it into her mouth.

I opened up the phone book and flicked through the pages until I found the section for exterminators. It was only until I opened the book properly that I noticed all the advertisements were moving. "The pictures are animated!" I said in amazement.

"Uh yeah," Zelda said as she scrolled through her phone, her cup of tea in her other hand. "Have you never seen a magical phone book before?"

"You're asking that question to the woman who only found she was a witch a month ago?" I asked.

"Fair point," Zelda conceded.

Zelda might have thought the magical phone book was

mundane, but I was very entertained. For a few minutes I forgot what I was even looking for and merely admired all the strange adverts, many of which I didn't understand at all. One advert had large flashing letters that read, *'Mispy Whallows in your attic? Call Jack Spratt now!'*

Another advert showed a short animation of a broom-wielding witch chasing gnomes around a garden. *'Martha Gloombarrow. Gnome-remover extraordinaire!'*

"There!" Hermes said, apparently reading the book over my shoulder. He jumped onto my lap and pawed at an advert for *'Bitz and Bosch – Professional Poxy Exterminators!'*

"Hang on a second," I said, looking up at Phoebe. "Bitz and Bosch. That's the appointment you just told me about fifteen minutes ago."

"Yes, it's scheduled for nine tomorrow morning."

"But how can that be possible. I haven't even called them yet!"

"Well, you haven't booked it yet. But it's going to happen," Phoebe said assertively.

I looked at Zelda. "She claims she *can't* see the future."

"Everyone knows that," Zelda said. "Time owls just have a broader perception of the present."

"Olaphax," Phoebe corrected. "Also, Zora, while you're in the phone book can you find me a perch or a cage? This kitchen table just won't cut it. If it's a perch, I would preferably like something made out of willow. If it's a cage it needs to be silver or white gold."

"Sure, she'll just find a phone number for a perch and see if it can come and live here!" Hermes mocked. He looked at me and rolled his eyes. "These time owls, they don't know it all!"

"Actually I was thinking more that Zora finds the number for a magical pet shop," Phoebe clarified.

"That... makes more sense," Hermes said quietly.

"I'll have a look in a moment, I promise. Let me call these guys first and see if I can get an appointment."

"You can," Phoebe said, once again calling on her knowledge of the future... or not-future. Whatever. I picked up my phone and dialed the number on the ad. After a few rings someone answered.

"Hallo? This is Bitz of *Bitz and Bosch*, professional Poxy removers and exterminators!" a man said in a high-pitched German accent.

"Hi, my name is Zora Wick, I live in Compass Cove, and I have just found a Poxy in my apartment. Could I employ your removal services?"

"Of course, of course, how bad are we talking here? Are there many about? What's the largest thing they have tried to take so far?"

"I've just caught one so far, or should I say my familiar caught one. They tried to take a kettle."

"A kettle?!" Bitz said in alarm. "Oh my, it is quite bad then already. We'll have to begin work at once. How large is ze property?"

"Just a regular two-bedroom apartment—but it is attached to a bakery as well. Does that factor in?"

"Have things gone missing from the bakery?" Bitz asked.

"Now that you mention it, yes. But just small things."

"Then it seems the entire property will need servicing. How does 9am tomorrow morning sound?"

I looked at Phoebe briefly. It was just as she said. "I think that can work. By the way, what are you going to do to these little guys? You're not going to kill them, are you?"

"That is what exterminators usually do," Bitz said plainly. "Don't be fooled by their humanoid appearance, Poxy are very nasty little creatures. Take it from a guy that's been cursed by them, you don't want any half-measures!"

"I just don't think it will sit well in my conscience if you genocide these things, even if they are a horrible nuisance."

"We do offer nonlethal extraction, but it will take longer, cost more, and there's no guarantee they won't come back. The best thing is to go scorched earth on these buggers. We can remove their burrows, but they follow scent back. Usually they don't, but we've had customers report Poxy coming back after several years."

"I think the nonlethal option works best for me. What can I say, I'm a gentle soul." I looked over at the Poxy in the glass jar, who was currently bent over with its cheeks spread as it mooned me. "But I may reconsider."

Bitz laughed. "Very well, give me your contact details and address, Miss Wick, and we shall be with you tomorrow morning. Oh, one more thing, for nonlethal extraction the property will have to be fumigated."

"Fumigated! I can't have my bakery fumigated! People will think I have roaches!"

"We can deal with the roaches too," Bitz offered.

"I don't have roaches. I run a very clean kitchen! I'm trying to say that I can't have a tent over the building. It will drive customers away!"

"Fear not, we can be very discreet. Though you will have to close your business during the process; it will take three days. You will also have to find somewhere else to stay during that time. Now, what's your address?"

After handing Bitz the information I put the phone down and sighed. "I have to close the bakery for three days, and find a place to crash," I said to no one in particular.

"Crash at my place, yay!" Zelda said. "Sister sleepover. It will be so exciting!"

"You sleep over here like three nights a week," I laughed. "It's hardly new! Constance won't be happy about the business closing for three days though, and we can't really take the financial hit right now. I'll have to take the van on the road to try and recoup the losses. I'll open up early tomorrow as well to try and sneak in some extra business before the work rush."

I then noticed Phoebe pulling a funny face—if it was even possible for an owl to pull a funny face. "What's that look about?" I asked.

"Can't tell you," she said.

"What do you mean you can't tell me?"

"A time owl can't tell you something about the future if it will change too many things," Zelda said, still scrolling away on her phone. "Something fun must be coming up for you tomorrow morning."

I looked at the owl, dreading whatever it was she had seen. "Just tell me!"

Phoebe shook her head. "Nope. Are you going to call a pet shop? I need a perch. Or a cage!"

"I need you to tell me what you saw! You're making me nervous about tomorrow morning!"

"Sorry, Zora, I just can't. You'll be fine anyway. Probably. Most likely."

I hung my head and sighed. "With friends like this…" I muttered to myself.

CHAPTER 3

The following morning I woke up early, and for someone that owns a bakery that is saying something. I normally opened the bakery at eight in the morning, but as *Bitz and Bosch* were coming along at nine to close me down for three days I was determined to get in as many hours as possible before I had to take my show on the road.

So I opened the bakery at six, hopeful that it might make a little difference. Honestly, I knew full well that most people weren't up at this hour and patrolling the streets for baked goods, but it couldn't hurt. That's what I kept telling myself as I poured another coffee and yawned at the empty shop.

"When are you going to hire an assistant?" my Aunt Constance said as her ghostly figure popped through the wall. I thought I would be used to her popping out of nowhere by now, but she had a gift for scaring the life out of people.

"Sweet mother of milk rolls!" I yelled, just stopping myself from spilling my coffee. "Can you please stop sneaking up on me like that?"

"Let an old witch have her thrills!" she complained. "Why are you open so early, and when are you going to get an assistant?"

"I have an assistant. I have two actually."

"Your cousins Zelda and Celeste don't count. They're already busy enough with their café. You need someone that can be here full-time to help you out."

"I'll put an ad in the paper today, okay? What else do you want from me?"

"Answers. Why are you open so early? No one comes in the bakery at this time. I mean you might get a few stragglers from the finance district; those guys wake up early, but they're all health nuts too—rare to see them in here."

I took a deep breath and sipped my coffee as I prepared to tell Constance that her bakery was going to be closed for three days. I'd inherited it a year after she died, and she was keen for things to get going again.

"We've got a Poxy problem. We have to close for three days. The exterminators are coming this morning at nine."

"Poxy! Oh for the love of—why does it take three days to get rid of Poxy?!"

"I asked them to do the nonlethal option."

Constance's mouth fell open as she stared at me in disbelief. "Why would you do that? They're Poxy! Just have them killed and be done with it! Much quicker!"

"That idea doesn't sit right with me, even if they are annoying. Where is the board marker? I'm sure I left if here somewhere…"

"Three guesses where that went," Constance said sarcastically. "Why can't you just let the exterminators snuff the little whippets? If you go soft on them, they come back."

"We're not killing them, okay? I just don't like the idea. I'm a Prismatic Witch, aren't I? Shouldn't my opinion count for something?"

"Pulling that card already, are we?" Constance said with an amused grin. "Fair enough, Zora, it's your call. You know money is tight at the moment though. This first month has been quieter than I would have hoped. And on top of that we're looking at three days with no sales…"

"No, we will have sales. I'm going to take the van out and bake and sell on the road."

"Now you're showing initiative!" Constance said with approval. "I won't write you off just yet, Zora."

"I thought you said I was the only person that could inherit this place and make it a success."

"Yes, well… I'm starting to think maybe that vision wasn't entirely correct!" I rolled my eyes and Constance floated over and patted her hand on my head. "Sorry, darling, that was mean. I know you've got it in you; goodness knows no one else in the town could handle the bakery. You're going to smash this, Zora; it will just take time. What are those? They look delicious."

"Rum and raisin swirls. I came up with them yesterday. You think they'll sell?"

"If they taste half as good as they look, yes. Ooh! A customer. I'll leave you to it. Adios!" With that, Constance launched through the ceiling and vanished. A second later the bakery door opened and a middle-aged man with snow-white hair walked in. He was wearing jeans and a blazer over a T-shirt. It looked as if he'd had a little work done on his face, because it was smooth and shiny like a Ken doll—not a line in sight. He had a phone in one hand, and he was holding it up in front of his chest.

"Alright you miserable lot, you voted for me to come in here, so let's have a look and see what it's about," he said, seemingly speaking to the screen on his phone. He approached the desk and looked up at me, whistling silently as he did so. "Good morning, sweetheart. My lovely followers just voted for me to come in here and find out why a bakery would be open at this ungodly hour. What's the story?"

"Early bird catches the worm," I said. "Are you uh… streaming this?"

"I am. Is that a problem? Fifty-nine people are staring at your beautiful mug right now. How old are you? Don't tell me. If you're under thirty it will never work. Let's just pretend you're thirty and it will do me fine."

"I have a boyfriend," I lied.

"Never stopped me before, cupcake." He winked. As he did so I felt my entire body recoil. This guy easily had thirty years on me, and he was hitting on me in such a sleazy manner. "Do you know what streaming is by the way?" he asked.

"Ye—" I began, but he immediately cut me off.

"So streaming is like a TV show, but I'm filming on my phone, and then people watch it live online, it's kind of like—" he mansplained.

"I know what streaming is," I said, throwing in another yawn for good measure.

"Don't interrupt me," the white-haired man said. "It's very unattractive when a woman interrupts a man. Now I—"

"Were you going to order something, or just stand here and talk all morning?"

"Excuse me?" the man said, looking up from his phone for the first time and meeting my eye. "I don't like your tone. Do you know who you're talking to?"

"Someone that wants to exchange money for a baked good?" I said sarcastically.

"I'm Mark Mobson, but you already know that of course. I don't need to tell you that I'm a big deal around here." Mark stood tall for a moment, a smug look upon his face.

"Um sure, of course you are. I've never heard of you, but good for you." Though my words were pleasant my tone was anything but. If this guy didn't order something in the next three seconds he'd be getting evicted from the bakery.

"Uh-oh guys," Mark said to his phone. "Looks like we've got another liar on our hands, another pretty young woman intimidated by a local legend. What do you say, do I put the moves on her? Vote in the chat now."

"I think it's time for you to leave," I said.

"Shut up a minute, love, I'm waiting on the vote to come in... and it's in! Alright, the chat overwhelmingly wants me to chat you up. Now, first of all you need to know about my list. I'm looking for a girlfriend, but there are rules."

"Oh, really?" I said, crossing my arms and tilting my head to the side. I had to admit I was intrigued now. It wasn't every day one came across such a raging narcissist, and I was curious to hear how insane this guy actually was.

"Rule number one, I'm in charge. What I say is final."

"Sounds reasonable," I snarked.

"Number two, you keep yourself in shape. You're not allowed a phone, and you're *not* allowed to talk to other guys. You have to be a good cook, you must like dogs, hate cats, love dance music and hate rock music. We also have to like the same TV shows; currently I'm watching—"

"I'm sorry, is this all for rule two? It's very long."

"So, what do you say?" Mark said, ignoring my question. "Let me take you out for a date. We can go to my club, *Angel*; it's the most happening place in this dreary little town. I just came from there actually after an all-night party."

"The most happening place?" I asked. "You sound like someone from the 1950s!" I then stared at him a moment, trying to decipher his true age under the plastic surgery burdened face. "Actually…"

"Tonight or tomorrow, pick one," he said sternly. "My chat is getting bored."

"I'm not coming to your club," I said. "And I'm not interested in a date. You're too old, and frankly you've got more red flags than the entire country of China."

For the second time Mark took his eyes off his phone and stared at me. This time the look was full of malice and irritation, but an amused smile flicked on his face. "It's a good thing chat thinks you're funny, darling; people don't talk to me like that and get away with it often."

"I think it's time you left," I said.

"I want to talk to your manager."

"Alright, let me get them." I walked through the door that led into the kitchen and came straight back into the bakery. "Hi, I'm the manager. Get out of my shop."

Mark Mobson threw his head back and laughed. "Ha! I like her! You have to admit she's got balls. Alright, let's order something and then I can get out of this miserable heap. I'll take a brownie."

Part of me just wanted to refuse the man's custom, but I reminded myself why I'd opened early, I needed extra sales to cover the closed period. "Fine, one brownie coming up." I walked towards the glass counter when Mark piped up again.

"No, not one that's been sitting in the cabinet. I want a fresh one, from the *back*."

I stared at him a moment and ground my teeth together. I had half a mind to cast a baseball-sized invisible magic projectile at his chest, but I kept it together. "The brownies in the cabinet were put out this morning, but you know what, I'll get one from the back."

I headed into the kitchen and grabbed a brownie off a tray that had just come out of the oven. They were still hot, too hot to eat, but if I was lucky the smooth-brained moron in the bakery would burn his mouth. I bagged up the brownie, went back into the front, and took his money.

"You have a good day now, beautiful," he said. "We'll see if chat votes for me to come back here again and get your number."

"Maybe they can vote for you to take a long walk off a short pier? Don't let the door hit you on the way out."

Thankfully Mark Mobson left without another word, and once he was gone I was glad to see the back of him. After that only two other people came in before my usual opening time, and fortunately they were much more pleasant. By the time nine came around I flipped the sign on the door to closed, put a note in the window, and posted a short message on my socials letting people know the bakery would be closed for the next three days.

Closed for renovations, we're on the road for three days in the van!

I'd just got back upstairs to the apartment when the buzzer sounded. "Yes?" I said.

"It's Bitz, of *Bitz and Bosch*, we're here for the appointment."

"Come up," I said as I buzzed them in. "Up the stairs on your left." I opened the apartment door and saw a short thin man in a suit walking up the stairs. He had a large brown moustache and thick eyeglasses.

"Would you like a drink?" I asked as I welcomed him into the apartment.

"I'll have a coffee, two sugars. Bosch will take a coffee too, no sugar for him."

Bitz set his suitcase down and let his gaze move across the apartment. I stood by the open door, waiting for this 'Bosch' to come up too. "Should I uh… leave the door open for him?" I asked, after a few seconds of no activity.

"Huh?" Bitz said, turning his head back to look at me. He was on his hands and knees, looking under a cabinet I used to store shoes. "Oh no, he'll be along shortly. So where has most of the activity been?"

"In the apartment mostly I'd say, though things have gone missing in the bakery downstairs too."

"There's a bakery downstairs, a kitchen, and the apartment up here?"

"That's right," I said, watching as he crawled along the floor like a dog following a scent. He stopped by a blank section of skirting board and tapped it with this finger, making a quiet sound with his mouth that suggested he'd found something of interest. "Yeah, there's Poxy here alright; there are traces of several burrows."

"There are?" I asked as I came over to the blank skirting board. "How can you tell? It looks normal to me."

"Move your fingers close, you'll feel the magic," he said. I did so and felt a faint vibration on my fingertips.

"I've still got the one I caught. It's in the jar on the table," I said, pointing him in the right direction.

"Ah, jolly good, that's very helpful. I can see what brood they're from." Bitz got up, walked over to the table and bent down to inspect the Poxy. The small creature was currently asleep.

"Brood?" I asked.

"Yes, Poxy live in large broods. There are currently fifteen known broods across America, they're all a little different. Some better, some worse. Just as I suspected," he said to himself after eyeing up the Poxy. "This isn't good. This little fella is from the Goon-Sach brood."

"Is that bad?"

"Yes, they're the worst type of Poxy. Very aggressive, and they work quickly. We'll have to get to work straight away. My goodness, that owl has the most amazing feathers," he said, looking up at Phoebe, who was currently asleep, perched on top of a bookcase.

"It's a time owl," I said. "Or Olaphax as she likes to be called."

"Remarkable," he said with wonder. "You've sorted accommodation, right? We can start in the next hour. Any animals will have to go too."

"Yeah, it's all sorted. I'll make your drink and then go and pack."

I left Bitz to it, sorted drinks for him and his absent colleague and then I packed my things. Hermes had fallen asleep in his cat carrier, so I just closed the door behind him. I packed myself a small suitcase and went back into the living room to place my things by the door. As I came around the corner, I nearly walked into a huge man that was all muscle.

"Argh!" I screamed, almost dropping my things. "Who are you?!"

"Bosch," he said in a deep voice.

"Oh, that makes sense." He stepped aside and I walked past him into the kitchen. "Where's the other guy?" I asked, setting my things down. As I turned around again, I saw Bitz standing in the spot where Bosch had just been. I stared for a moment, finding myself quite confused. "Am I going mad?"

"Mad?" Bitz asked. "Why ever do you ask that?"

"I could have sworn you were just a seven-foot-tall skinhead made of muscle."

"This guy?" With those words Bitz suddenly transformed into the behemoth 'Bosch', who waved a hand at me and then transformed back into Bitz. I closed my mouth and shook my head.

"I have to cut out the coffee," I said to myself.

"I take it you've never heard of a geminus?" Bitz asked. "We are rare, but most amongst the magical community are aware of our kind."

"I'm a new witch," I said. "Only a month into this madness. What's a geminus?"

"Sometimes when twins are born in a magical family, they are born into... the same person."

"That is utterly bizarre," I remarked. "So, you share a body?"

"More like we share a space," Bitz explained. "We are permanently tethered to one another, like two sides of the same coin. Only one can ever come out, though we can switch between each person freely. Some people call geminus, 'were-people'."

"So you're both twins? But you're so..."

Bitz transformed into the goliath Bosch again. "Different? Yes, geminus are usually opposites in every way. I do the heavy lifting." He snapped back into the form of his smaller brother, Bitz.

"And I do the thinking," Bitz said. "Together, we make quite the duo."

"Well... you learn something new every day!" I remarked, throwing in a nervous laugh for good measure. Bitz did not laugh in return. "Anyway... I'm all packed now. I'll just grab Phoebe and get out of your hair."

"Very good. We'll call if we need to get in touch; this should be a fairly straightforward job though."

"What do you do with them by the way?" I asked.

"I beg your pardon?" Bitz asked.

"The Poxy. If you're not going to kill them then what do you do with them?"

"We drive them out into the wilderness and dump them near a brood burrow. Bosch and I have spent several decades mapping these vermin and their network of magical burrows. Once they're out there it will take some time for them to get back to civilization—but they *will* come back, maybe not to your apartment, but someone else's house, for sure."

With that I grabbed Phoebe and loaded my things into Constance's mobile kitchen van. The van—which Constance had named 'Helen'— was a bright pink monstrosity with a giant cupcake mounted to the roof, the sides of the van decorated in stars and cakes. Constance had fitted this thing out with a mini kitchen in the back so she could bake and sell around town, but she'd always been too nervous to actually take the van out because it was so big.

I didn't have that anxiety however and had no problems pulling the pink cupcake tank onto the roads of Compass Cove. Zelda's apartment was just a few minutes away, but I'd agreed to pick her up from Celeste's café first, so I turned onto the road and set off. Sister pickup, here we come!

CHAPTER 4

"*P*lease get that giant pink monstrosity away from the front of my business," my cousin Celeste said, a look of sheer horror upon her face as I walked into her café. Celeste was a kitchen witch just like her mother, though her talents lent themselves more to cooking savory things instead of baking; that's why she never took over Constance's bakery.

"What's wrong with it?!" I said, coming to Helen's defense. "Leave Helen alone. This is only her second real outing in Compass Cove!"

"You called that thing Helen?" Celeste said. Celeste was short and round. What she lacked in height she made up in sass. "It looks like Frankenstein and Barbie got together, fooled around in a neon-paint factory, and gave birth to that monster."

"Actually, your mother named it Helen. I'm just following her example. I would never name a vehicle 'Helen'; it doesn't seem right to me."

"Change it then! Don't let my mom boss you around from beyond the grave!"

"That's kind of our whole relationship though," I jokingly pointed out. "I run her business, she appears out of nowhere, scares the crap out of me, and tells me what I'm doing wrong."

"I really wish she'd stop doing that—the sudden appearance thing. She floated through the wall this morning while I was getting dressed after the shower! I was halfway into a pair of tights and I nearly fell down the stairs. The stairs, Zora! You have to have a word with her."

"Me!? Why me?! She's your mom!"

"I haven't thought up a good reason, but I've got like really good intuition, and it tells me that you're the one that has to put her in her place," Celeste said vaguely, adding a nod as though it cemented her position.

"Hmm... and the award for least convincing argument goes to..."

"Finished! Let's hit the road!" Zelda said as she came through the back door of the café. Her shift was over with, and she was ready to go. She fist-bumped Celeste before ducking under the counter to join me on the customer side.

"Don't forget you're in early tomorrow," Celeste said to Zelda. "I've got that thing in town I have to do."

"Sounds awfully specific," I said.

"It's a date," Zelda said to me. "Whenever she gets vague it's because she has a date."

"Ooh, a date!" I said animatedly. "Who's the lucky guy!"

"I do not have a date," Celeste grumbled, turning a bright shade of pink as she did so. "It's an appointment with my... foot doctor," she lied, rather unconvincingly.

"The only foot she's going to be seeing is the one in this guy's pants, eh, eh?" Zelda said as she nudged me playfully with her elbow.

"What in the sweet monkey Moses are you talking about?" I said, half-laughing as I stared at my bemusing sister.

"That didn't really land, did it?" she said, reflecting on her foot pants joke.

"No," Celeste said flatly. "No, it didn't."

"A date though, that's exciting! You aren't going to give us any details?" I said to Celeste.

"No, because there are no details to give, and every time I have a date Zelda and Sabrina show up and ruin it, so I'm keeping it to myself!" Celeste said.

"So, there *is* a date," Zelda said, throwing in an immature high-pitched cooing sound for good fun. "You can tell when she's lying. She always goes with the foot doctor excuse, and she blushes like wild."

"Just like you, beetroot face," Celeste pointed out. "Now get out my café and stay out of my personal life. It's nunya!"

"It's what now?" Zelda asked, her forehead creasing in confusion.

"Nunya business!" Celeste said, cackling at catching Zelda out. Her amusement faded quickly, and a serious expression came over her. "Seriously though, get out. I've got work to do and you're wasting my time. Bye!"

THOUGH I HAD BRIEFLY BEEN to Zelda's apartment a few times while living here in Compass Cove, I had never stayed over for the night before. Compass Cove was a pretty little town, with lots of buildings originating from the Art Deco era of architecture. Apparently, the town held the record for most historical buildings in the whole of the states, and it really did look like a postcard on almost every street.

Zelda's place was on the far west side of town, about a ten-minute drive from Constance's bakery. She lived in an apartment block, a hundred-year-old building that was perplexingly narrow, but also quite long.

"I never really noticed the weird shape of this building before now," I said to Zelda as I set my things down in the spare room. I opened the cat carrier, only to find that Hermes was still sleeping. Phoebe flew up to a bookshelf and settled herself rather quickly. The guest room was not exactly roomy, it was just wide enough to fit a double bed, but long enough that it could fit another three beds length-to-length.

"Yeah, this was one of the last buildings put up in Compass Cove. There wasn't much room left, so they squeezed it in between two blocks; that explains the narrow shape."

We headed back into the living room, which again was narrow and long. The couch and the TV were nearly pressed together, and you basically had to shuffle past to squeeze through.

"It's almost like living inside a giant pencil," I remarked.

Zelda laughed. "Yeah, I should probably find something a bit more normal. I don't know what was going through my mind when I bought this place. I guess I was drawn by the allure of having the penthouse."

"This is the penthouse?!" I said in disbelief.

"Yeah, it actually used to belong to the old station master; it's right above Ligo Street station. He personally overlooked the design of this building and had iron rods put in the walls. They run from the station all the way up to the penthouse, so he could always feel if the trains were running on time."

That was another amusing fact about Compass Cove; it was one of the smallest towns in America with a functioning subway system, built largely because a woman from a wealthy railway family ended up settling here.

Without even looking at her watch Zelda held a finger up. "Wait for it."

A second later the apartment started shaking violently. Plates rattled in the kitchen, ornaments shuffled across shelves, the lights swung from the ceiling and dust trickled down too. "What was that?!" I said, half-fearing an earthquake.

"That's the 11:36 from Hadish Square. Right on time!" she said cheerily.

I stared at my sister in dismay. "Zelda… what on earth compelled you to buy this place?"

"Well, I like places with character. And you have to admit, this apartment has character by the bucket full."

"How pushy was the realtor?" I asked.

"Oh very. You know what I'm like. I'd barely taken three steps in this place when I proclaimed my love for it."

"But you don't love it," I said.

"I didn't then, but I didn't want to disappoint the realtor. He was so nice, and he was just trying to do his job. He showed me photographs of his kids. I bet the bonus he got from this sale went a long way to making those kids happy."

"He's a realtor," I said flatly. "He probably stole those photos off the internet. Zel, why have you got to be such a pushover?"

"I just don't like disappointing people, and this place has grown on me." Just then the apartment started shaking wildly again. Zelda smiled. "11:42, Ligo Street to the Hospital station."

"We *have* to find you a new place," I said.

Her smile faltered a little bit. "Yeah, probably. The roof terrace is nice though."

"Go on then, indulge my curiosity." I followed Zelda back to the front door of the apartment. She opened a door that I thought was a closet, revealing a narrow set of stairs that led up. I followed her up on to the roof to find a pleasantly open roof terrace, complete with a little garden and patio furniture.

"Zelda, this is much nicer! I bet this is lovely in the summer!" At the moment, in the dead of winter, it was bitter up here; we were ten stories up after all and the wind was bracing. Snowflakes were beginning to fall through the air.

"Oh, it is. I spend most of my time up here when it's warm out, and the view is good too." I followed her over to a wall at the edge of the roof and looked out across the town of Compass Cove. To our right was the lake itself, and on its shores, I could make out the distant outlines of the other three towns surrounding the water. "Gosh, that wind has taken the heat right out of me already," I said, starting to shiver.

"Same, let's head back down and I'll make us some cocoa." I followed Zelda back downstairs and we squeezed into her matchbook kitchen to have cocoa around the table. "What's on your agenda for today then?" she asked me while joining me at the table. I took my cocoa and had a sip.

"Hm. Delicious. Agenda for today, hm, well I suppose we should take the van out on the road and start selling some baked goods."

"We?" Zelda said with a querying brow. I hadn't actually yet asked her if she would help, I'd just sort of assumed. I gave her my sweetest smile in effort to win her over.

"If my most beautiful little sister would be so inclined to help of course," I said.

"I was planning on sitting in and playing Breath of the Wild all day, but I guess I could always bring my Nintendo with me and play during quiet moments."

"Atta girl," I said, letting my eyes wander across the dinky kitchen. The wall besides the table was full of framed pictures containing all sorts of art. Right next to us there was an illustration of an owl on a branch, with a large moon behind it. "That reminds me, Phoebe asked me to sort out a cage or a perch for her. Do you know of any magical pet shops in town?"

"There's a small place a few blocks from here, but honestly the best pet shop around Compass Cove is in Wildwood on the west coast." Of the four towns around the lake, I'd only actually been to two so far, Sacketsville on the south coast, and Compass Cove town on the north coast. The roads around the lake were currently washed out after a landslide, and the only way across the water was by ferry.

"Wildwood, what's that like?" I asked.

"It has a bit of a bad reputation because it's a little poorer, farms, trailer parks, that sort of thing—Wildwood has a very strong community though. I grew up there, it's a perfectly fine town—definitely a little more country than Compass Cove though."

"And what about Eureka?" I asked. One handy thing about Compass Cove was that the names of the towns around the lake matched their position on the lake. Sacketsville was on the south shore, Wildwood on the west. Eureka was on the east. The only anomaly was Compass Cove itself, which was on the north. Apparently, our family was directly descended from the ancestors that founded the town and broke the naming convention. The Wick family knew how to wind people up even back then.

"Eureka is almost the exact opposite. There's a college there, and the Flight Center too, some computer labs too. A lot of smart people with book learning. Liza actually lives in Eureka. She's on some 'terribly-important' magic council or something like that. Her personal life is a bit of a mystery to be honest."

"And Sacketsville?" I asked.

"Mostly just a normal town. Lots of humans, and lots of water-sports. If you want good old mortal fun that's your place. It becomes a bit of a party town in the summer months."

"So, the best pet shop is in Wildwood?" I asked.

"Yes, Zambo's Pet Store. He's got everything. A lot of people in Wildwood won't deal with folk from out of a town, but you'll probably get a free pass because you're with me."

"Why all the animosity?"

"The towns around the lake haven't really got on well in years, and lots of it comes down to the feud between the Wicks and the Brewers; they're two of the oldest magical families around Compass Cove, but they don't get on very well."

When I first moved here and found out Zelda was my sister, we spent many nights staying up and talking to one another, catching up on a lifetime of events. Zelda and I shared the same mother—a mysterious witch that was currently missing—but our fathers were different.

I was raised by my father, a human man, on the west coast. Zelda's father was a man named 'Billy Brewer' who was apparently something of a hillbilly type, belonging to the 'infamous' Brewer family.

"Ooh, does that mean we can go and visit the rest of your family?!" I said excitedly. So far, I'd only met the Wick part of my lineage in Compass Cove. The elusive hillbilly Brewers had evaded me.

Zelda pulled a funny face at the idea. "Um yeah, maybe? I mean they're very busy, so probably not," she said evasively.

"Right," I said, wondering why that seemed like a sensitive topic for Zelda. "I suppose I should call ahead first and see if they actually stock said items. Do you have a number for them?"

"No, but you can check the phone book."

"Right, how do I summon that. I saw Hermes do it the other day."

"Oh, it's easy. You don't even need magic!" she said, drawing in a large breath to shout. "You just shout, 'Phone book!'"

Before I could stop her, a magical portal opened on the kitchen wall, and the heavy tome flew through the air and walloped me in the side of the head. It knocked me off-balance and I nearly fell out of my chair. As I straightened up, I had a look on my face that could curdle milk. Zelda was sipping her cocoa and staring out of the window, oblivious that she had nearly just concussed me.

"This family…" I muttered under my breath, after having been clobbered a second time by the magic phone book in twenty-four hours.

"Huh?" Zelda asked.

"Nothing," I muttered back. "Hurry up and finish your cocoa. We're taking the van on the road and heading into the town center before we miss the lunch rush. You're going to be on the register!"

"Aww!" she protested.

"Quit yer whining," I said. "You're lucky I don't send you out solo!"

"What did I do wrong?!" she wailed.

CHAPTER 5

I didn't have much of a plan for the mobile bakery van; I just decided to head to the busiest square and park up, hoping I'd catch the footfall of office folk as they headed out for their daily lunch. Although it was cold the streets of Compass Cove were generally always quite busy. The local town was thriving for small businesses, and people made a point to get out every day and browse the various wares for sale.

As soon as we pulled up, I decided to put a message out on our socials. *Hey, Zora from Sugar Rush here, we're on the road today in the van, and we just pulled up in Grimwick Square. Come down and grab a bite, we're here for the next hour!*

"Why just an hour?" Zelda asked.

"The illusion of scarcity," I said. "If people nearby think we'll be here all day, then there's no urgency. If we give them a timeline that puts a fire under their butts."

Zelda stared at me in an impressed way. "You might actually be better at this business stuff than you give yourself credit for."

"Forbes Magazine, here I come," I joked.

Little did I anticipate, the mobile bakery van was actually a roaring success. At our first location we were swept off our feet as tides of lunch-seeking workers lined up for a sweet bite to accompany their meals. I'd prepared a lot of stock to drive around with us as baking obviously took time, but we were rapidly flying through my prepared goods, so I had to hop into the back and break in the mobile kitchen, cooking up scones and cookies—things I could batch cook in twenty minutes to replenish our shelves.

After the first location we hit up three more locales, and each time we arrived I pinged another message on our socials, letting people know where we were, and that we'd only be there for an hour.

"Oh gosh!" an excited woman in nurse scrubs said as she ran up to the van when we were parked outside the hospital. "I've been watching your feed all day, hoping you'd stop by the hospital! I had to take a break early, I was worried I'd miss you. Can I get a brownie?"

"We have scones and cookies left," Zelda said, parroting a line she'd already told a hundred other customers today. We'd both been flying around the interior of the van nonstop since we'd set off, and we were drenched with sweat and feeling tired.

"I'll take both," the woman said eagerly.

"Here you go," I said, handing her the order. "We'll have more things baked ahead of tomorrow. We didn't anticipate the van would be such a hit."

"It's a godsend! See you tomorrow!" the customer said cheerily.

By the time we'd finished doing rounds of the town it was nearly seven in the evening. We drove back to Zelda's apartment and crashed on the couch, both too tired to say much more.

"Crumbs on a cracker," she groaned. "That was harder than I thought it would be."

"You're telling me," I said as I stared up at the ceiling. "I haven't had that much custom since I took over the bakery. There might be more to this van business than meets the eye."

"You know I've got to cover Celeste in the café tomorrow. There's no way you can do that all by yourself; you seriously need to hire an assistant," Zelda said.

"Yeah, I know. I'll have to struggle for one day, as I'm not going to find an assistant in time for tomorrow. Where are you going?" I said as Zelda pushed herself up from the couch.

"I'm having a bath and going to bed. I'm exhausted!"

"Don't you want dinner?" I asked.

"I'm going to eat a microwave meal in the bath. Feel free to judge me."

"Hey, no judgments here, sister. You go and live your best life. To be honest I'm tempted to do the same thing when you're finished!"

Zelda nodded sleepily and snapped finger guns at me as she left the room, heading towards the kitchen. As she did so the apartment started to tumble again, dust trickling down from the ceiling. "8:26 from Ligo Street!" she shouted to me from the kitchen. Ah yes. I'd forgotten about the trains.

Shortly after Zelda locked herself in the bathroom her apartment buzzer sounded. I peeled myself off the couch to answer it. "Yes?" I said.

"Yo, it's Sabrina. You eaten yet?"

"No, I'm recovering after my day."

"Buzz me in. I've got a treat for you."

A few minutes later Sabrina came into the apartment holding a casserole dish covered in foil. "Surprise, I made you guys some dinner! It's lamb curry. I've been following your socials all day and thought you might be hungry. I'm not as good a cook as the rest of the family, but I can whip up a good curry—if I do say so myself."

My entire mouth filled with saliva, and I welcomed Sabrina in. She was Celeste's sister. Out of all of us she was the tallest, and she was the only one that wasn't a kitchen witch, though I *suppose* I technically wasn't either.

"I think you just got elevated to number one cousin," I said jokingly. "Come in. Let's eat. Zelda's in the bath with a microwave meal."

"Figures," Sabrina snorted.

We both squeezed ourselves into Zelda's pokey kitchen table and I positively devoured at least three quarters of the curry. I hadn't even realized how hungry I was, but the food definitely restored a warmth in me. "I think there might be a little kitchen witch in you after all," I said with a satisfactory sigh as I sank back in my chair after setting my fork down.

Zelda came into the kitchen wrapped in a towel, her nose sniffing out the scent of the lamb curry. "Aw man," she said, pouting. "If I knew you were coming over, I would have waited for some real food!"

"Sorry," Sabrina said. "I would have messaged, but I thought it would make a nice surprise. It looks like you guys had a busy day today! I figured you could use a little help."

"You want to know if we have gossip on Celeste, don't you?" Zelda said with a smirk.

"That too," Sabrina admitted. "We were talking on the phone earlier and she was acting super sketchy. Said she had an appointment with a foot doctor tomorrow. Who's the boy?"

"We don't know," Zelda said. "But it's killing us too. She definitely has a date that she's hiding from us."

"Why don't you guys just let her date in peace?" I asked. They both looked at me like I'd suggested launching ourselves off the roof.

"Uh, because whenever one of us has a date Celeste is a nightmare too. She can't keep her nose out!" Sabrina protested.

"Be the change you want to see in the world?" I suggested.

"Nah, this is her comeuppance for being a nosy little shrew," Zelda said. "All the women in our family are like this, Zora. You'll get used to it."

"Yeah," Sabrina said, taking Zelda's side. "And what about you? When are we shifting your love life into gear? Didn't that undercover police hunk give you his phone number?"

"Hudson? Yes, he did, but it was more of a work arrangement."

"I think the only arranging he wants to do is putting himself on top of you," Zelda said. Both Sabrina and I looked at her, perplexed.

"I have never met anyone worse at innuendos than you," Sabrina said. "Like how are you even that bad at them? It doesn't make any sense."

"Leave me alone!" she moaned. "They're hard!"

"Maybe stop doing them then?" I laughed.

"So, spill the beans. What's going on with you and this dreamy *Hudson*?" Sabrina pressed, letting his name roll off her tongue like it was an exotic wine.

"Nothing. I haven't even spoken to him since everything went down. I haven't even thought about him!"

That was a lie. When I first moved here a month ago, I very quickly found myself involved in the midst of a murder plot. It turned out my Aunt Constance hadn't just dropped dead but had been poisoned. After some sleuthing I deduced the culprit was Marjorie Slade, a witch that ran a rival bakery just a few streets down from Constance's place.

There was a final showdown with Marjorie at her place, and things got pretty ugly. She took Zelda hostage and was threatening her. Things took a turn for the better at the last moment when the mysterious Hudson swung through a window and took Marjorie out—like some one-man SWAT team.

Up until then, Hudson—who I thought was just some outlaw biker—had actually been one of my suspects. He confided in me secretly afterwards, he was actually an undercover cop… or I supposed 'Agent' was a better word. He represented some secret organization, a magical group that called themselves 'MAGE'.

Since then, I'd heard nothing from Hudson, or this mysterious 'MAGE' group, but I had thought about him every single day, wishing I could see him again, and speak to him. Since the incident, he had vanished, like a ghost. He wasn't at the local park anymore, where he'd been in deep cover acting as an outlaw biker, and I hadn't seen him anywhere else in town.

"Look at her, totally zoning out," Zelda said, her voice bringing me out of my daydream. "I bet she's fantasizing about him naked."

"I know I would!" Sabrina said.

"Alright, alright, let's move onto a new topic. I'm done talking about my love life!"

"Boo!" Zelda said. I gave her a look and she shrank back. "Just kidding. I'm super tired anyway. Are you hanging around, Sabrina?"

"Nah, your apartment is way too small Zel. No offense, but it sets my claustrophobia off, plus the constant shaking makes me feel—" Sabrina paused as the entire apartment started rumbling once more, another train evidently passing below. "Seasick. We *have* to find you a new place, right, Zora?"

"Already on it. I don't know how I'm going to spend the next three days here."

"You could always give Hudson a call and see if you can spend the night with him?" Zelda said in a childish schoolgirl voice. I jumped up from the table, ready to show my little sister a thing or two.

"Right, I think someone is in dire need of a noogie! Come here!" I said as I chased her out of the kitchen.

"I was joking! I was joking!" Zelda shrieked while running away.

* * *

Not long after that Sabrina made her way home and Zelda went to bed. After a quick bath I crawled into bed also, exhausted after the long day. The trains thankfully stopped running after eleven at night. Admittedly I was a little worried the apartment would be shaking around the clock.

I'd only been asleep for a few hours when I woke to the sound of my phone buzzing on the bedside table. Blinking at the bright light of the screen I picked it up and answered the call.

"Hello?" I said groggily.

"Hey, Zora, it's Sabrina. This is totally embarrassing but I need your help."

"What time is it?" I said, pushing myself up in bed.

"Just after two in the morning," she answered. "Were you asleep?"

"Uh yeah, dude, what's going on?"

"I had to run out of town to pick up some stock for my shop. I'm at the self-storage on I-54, about fifteen minutes out of town."

"Why are you picking up stuff for work at two in the morning?" I groaned.

"I didn't mean to stay here this late, I just lost track of time!" she snapped.

"Alright, calm down, what's the problem?"

"My car won't start, and I've tried all the magic I can think of, but the engine is kaput. I already called Celeste and Zelda, but their phones must be on do not disturb. Can you do me a favor and come and pick me up?"

I could already tell from feel alone that my eyes were bloodshot. I was darn tired, but Sabrina was my cousin and she needed help. What other choice was there?

"I'll come and pick you up," I said. "Can you text me the address?"

"Sure, I'll ping it over right now. Thanks, you're a godsend, Zora."

I put my phone down and took a moment to compose myself before swinging out of bed and pulling on some clothes. I found Hermes in the living room watching the TV. "What are you doing up at this hour?" he asked.

"Winning the cousin of the year award." I went over to Zelda's door and knocked on it gently. It was slightly ajar, so I pushed it open. The light from the living room cut a wedge into the dark bedroom, revealing the less-than-graceful image of Zelda sleeping in her bed, drooling all over the place.

"Zel, I've got to go and pick up Sabrina; her car broke down."

Zelda made a mumbling sound in response but didn't open her eyes. "Don't forget to give the polar bear his dishwasher."

I nodded to myself; I don't know what else I expected. "You're completely useless," I said as I pulled the door closed again. I left the apartment, made my way down to the van, and copied the address of the self-storage place into my phone. Fifteen minutes later the directions had me turn off the highway and follow a dirt track into the wilderness.

"Where the heck is this place, Sabrina?" I muttered to myself. "Isn't there a self-storage place a little closer to town?!" According to my phone it was just on the left in a few hundred yards. The headlights from my van barely touched the night, but I could see the silhouette of a building up ahead. As I got closer, I realized it was an old, abandoned gas station.

Maybe the alarm bells should have been ringing at that point, but honestly, I think I was just too tired to function, I pulled into the old lot, grabbed my phone, and called Sabrina. Her phone went straight to voicemail. I tried again but found the same result.

I got out of the van and braced against the chill of the night. It was then that I saw five women in black hoods standing ten feet behind the van. I jumped back immediately.

"What's going on here?" I asked. "Where's Sabrina?"

"Where's Sabrina?" one of them said, copying my voice perfectly. The voice then shifted, until it sounded just like Sabrina. "Hi, I can't get to the phone right now, I'm sleeping, but please leave a message after the tone, beep!"

I realized then that I'd fallen for a trap. Sabrina hadn't called me at all. My fingertips began to crackle with the vibration of magic. The five women standing across from me were all witches. "Who are you?" I asked.

"We are the Sisters of the Shade, and we would like to speak with you, Zora Wick," the woman in the center of the group said.

I balled my hands into fists and swallowed at the nerves in my throat. I didn't have a good feeling about this at all. I was up the creek without a paddle. The aura coming off these women was dark.

"Okay," I croaked. "So… let's talk."

CHAPTER 6

"First of all, let me apologize for bringing you all the way out here at this late hour," the woman in the center said. She pulled back the hood of her robe, revealing the face of a dark brunette who couldn't be much older than me. Her features were sharp, her eyes cat-like. "Circumstances are unusual, and we have to operate in unusual ways. My name is Morgantha Hollow; this is my coven." She gestured to the women on either side of her.

"Okay, Morgantha Hollow. Why did you trick me into coming out here in the middle of the night, and what do you want from me?" I said, finding myself extremely suspicious of this woman and her 'coven'.

"We are part of a larger coalition, The Sisters of the Shade. We learned of your existence recently and are very interested in having you on our team," Morgantha explained.

"And why is that exactly?" I asked. I figured this had something to do with me being a Prismatic Witch, but so far only the women in my family knew about that, and I was under the impression we were keeping it a secret. I wasn't going to volunteer any information to this group of mysterious witches; they didn't need any more advantages—there were five of them and one of me.

"I think we both know the answer to that one," Morgantha said through an unsettling smile. "You're a Prismatic Witch, a true rarity. Although you are a new witch, the raw potential hiding inside of you is fierce. I can feel it."

"Prismatic Witch?" I said, deciding to play dumb. "I don't know what that is, and I don't know why you think that has anything to do with me."

Morgantha laughed to herself quietly, cackling like a witch from an old horror movie. "You're a rather convincing liar, but unfortunately for you I have a Raven." Morgantha pointed at the woman standing on her right. The mocha-skinned girl pulled back her hood, revealing to eyes that were shining white.

"I'm Raven. Can't see a thing except for the future," she said. "I saw a vision of you. A Prismatic Witch, right here in Compass Cove. I saw you picking your wand with your cousin Sabrina."

"Well... I can't lie my way out of that one. What are you, dark witches?" I asked. I had no idea if dark witches were actually a thing or not, but the vibe coming off these girls didn't exactly scream wholesome Christian gals.

"Dark is such an ugly word," Morgantha said. "We are simply witches that aren't afraid to pursue the full width of the magical spectrum."

"That definitely sounds like the sort of ambiguous thing an evil witch would say," I pointed out.

"Dark, evil, black magic, call it what you want," Morgantha said with a flippant shrug of her shoulder. "I don't know what that family of yours has told you, but I can assure you there's nothing wrong with pursuing the next level of magic."

"My family haven't really told me anything," I said. "I guess you girls are just giving off a bad vibe, that's all. I don't really dig it, so I think I'll be going now—"

"This path gives strength that the conventional methods can't bring," Morgantha said suddenly. "Each of us is blessed with a unique gift in return for our servitude. Raven can see the future, Lyre can copy any voice."

The girl on Morgantha's left pulled back her hood, revealing a baby-faced teen with curly blonde ringlets. "Lyre can copy any voice," she said, perfectly imitating Morgantha.

"I'm super interested to hear the roundup on everyone's magic power," I said sarcastically, "but as it's the middle of the night I'm going to head home and try to get some sleep before I have to be up for work tomorrow." I'd barely taken a step to the van when Morgantha cut in again.

"Imagine what gift would be bestowed upon someone like you, a Prismatic Witch? You could be strong. The strongest witch to ever live." With the words I saw Morgantha's eyes flash with greed, or some sort of strange power lust. Whatever it was, I didn't like it.

"Look, y'all pitched your black magic cult, and you've all got special powers, which I'll admit is kind of dope, but I'm not really interested in selling my soul to some dark lord so I can taste chocolate whenever it rains, or whatever." I paused in reflection. "Though *that* would be pretty useful around here."

"I think you're mistaken to the nature of this meeting," Morgantha said through a smile that was cordial, though growing sinister with each passing second. She took a step forward and her four companions followed. "You're going to come willingly, or we can take you. You might be a Prismatic Witch, but you have next to no training. It won't be difficult to overpower you."

"Right, but you're forgetting one thing," I said, desperately stalling for time, my heart now racing in my chest.

"Oh?" Morgantha replied, cocking her head to one side. "And what's that?"

"I have..." In that moment I pulled my wand out. I had absolutely nothing. The few spells Sabrina had taught me had gone straight out of my head. The only thing I was drawing was blanks.

"Enough of this, get her!" Morgantha shrieked. Without warning the five witches lunged forward. I let out a startled shriek, went to run away and instantly fell back on my ass. As I did so, a strong surge blasted out of the end of my wand. I felt a wall of force explode forward and it sent the five witches tumbling up and back by about fifteen feet—the hit took them by surprise just as much as it did me.

"What the heck?!" I gasped to myself, looking at my wand. I scrambled to my feet and ran to the van, only to find the door locked. "Keys, keys, keys!" I said, patting my pockets as I desperately tried to find them. Looking back across the lot I saw the keys on the ground. I ran over to grab them and saw the five dark witches back on their feet, running towards me.

"Don't let her get away!" Morgantha screamed.

With no time to get to the keys I decided to book it and started running in the direction of the old gas station. I cut around the corner and wondered what my next move was when I saw one of the dark witches had somehow ran around the other side to cut me off.

"Blink," she said. As she did so she teleported forward another five feet. "We all have a power."

"Still not interested!" I said, spinning on my heels to run back in the direction I'd come from. Straightaway I saw another of the dark witches behind me. Her form grew in a split second, until she was a hulk of muscle nearing six feet tall.

"We can do this the hard way if you want," the giant figure said, pounding a fist into her hand. Just then Morgantha came around the corner. Looking back over my shoulder I saw the other three witches behind me. I was fully surrounded.

"There's no chance this is all just to reach out about my car's extended warranty?" I joked, trying to stall for more time.

"Enough. Bag her up, Jenny. I don't want to hear another word out of her."

The huge, muscled witch stepped forward, pulling a small black cloth bag out of her robes. "No hard feelings," she said in her deep voice. "Just busi—"

All of a sudden a black blur came out of nowhere and crushed the huge witch into the concrete wall at the back of the old gas station. Next thing the blur careened into Morgantha and the witch with the white eyes. It came barreling towards me and I braced for impact but instead of attacking me it swept me up from the ground and we launched over the gas station in one giant bound.

"Get her!" I heard Morgantha shout from the other side of the building. "Don't let her get away!"

The thing carrying me landed on the ground and I realized it had swung me over its shoulder like a caveman hauling a kill back to its cave. It sprinted forward to a bike that was now parked near my van and quickly set me down on the ground. As it did so I finally saw the face of my savior, a huge muscle-bound man with long dark hair that was like a mane, a jaw that could break diamonds and dark brown eyes set under a strong and masculine brow.

"Who are you and what are you doing here?!" I gasped.

"Name's Blake," he said and swung his leg over the chopper. He turned the throttle and the engine roared to life. "And I'm here to save your ass. Get on. We'll grab the van in the morning."

"But I—"

"Get on," he ordered. No part of me wanted to argue with that tone, so I hopped on and a second later the bike was screaming away into the night. Looking back, I saw the five witches giving up the chase.

I'd made it out alive, but at what cost?

For the duration of the ride, I was terrified Morgantha and her cronies would chase after us, but after the initial tussle at the gas station I didn't see another sign of them. I held tight on the bike, wondering who this stranger was that had come to save me, and why exactly he'd been there at the right moment and the right time.

His chopper followed the north road that led back down to Compass Cove town, but before entering the town proper he pulled onto a side road and took his bike up a dirt track that ended at a cabin. He killed the engine and we both climbed off. "This is me," he said. "Let's get inside. Be quick about it."

Part of me wondered if perhaps I should show some hesitancy

about entering a stranger's cabin in the middle of nowhere, especially in the middle of the night, but my intuition told me this guy could be trusted—or at least I thought he could.

"I thought you were taking me home?"

"Isn't your home currently under magical fumigation?" he asked.

I raised a querying brow and took a step back. "And how would you, a complete stranger, know that?"

"You're going to have to take a leap of faith for a moment here and trust me. I know that's probably asking a lot of you," he said flippantly, turning around and walking up the front steps of the cabin. He unlocked the front door and pushed it open, turning around as if waiting for me to follow.

"What's that supposed to mean?" I asked.

"I don't know if you failed to notice, but I just saved your life back there. If someone did that for me, it would firmly put them in the 'safe to trust' column in my head."

"What do you want, thanks? I just got attacked by a crazy group of dark witches. I'm a little shaken. I think I can be forgiven after watching some guy move at supersonic speed, only to swing me over his shoulder and drive me to a cabin in the middle of nowhere."

"I can't take you back to your sister's place, not yet," he said. "I have to check it's safe first."

Again I took another step back. "How do you know I'm staying at my sister's place? Have you been following me?"

"Yes," he said plainly.

"So, you *are* a stalker." I pulled my wand out, ready to defend myself. It turned out this guy was crazy after all.

"No, it's my job to follow you. I'm your keeper."

"My what now?"

"Get inside the cabin and I'll explain," he said, his tone conveying that he had little time for any more questions. "I've got a lot to do tonight and not a lot of time left to do it, so do me a favor and just do as I say."

"Or what?" I asked. "You'll make me?"

He titled his head from side to side as he weighed up the consideration. "If that's how you want to play it." He took a step forward and then stopped and sighed. "Look, all I'm asking of you is five minutes. I can explain who I am and what I'm doing here, but we can't talk out here; it's not safe. I'm pretty sure one of those witches has got super hearing or some crazy nonsense like that."

I cast my mind back to Morgantha and her troupe of dark witches. They all had some sort of unique power; Morgantha said it was a reward for the dark path they had taken. It was entirely possible one of them could eavesdrop a conversation from miles away.

"If they can overhear a conversation from that far away then the flimsy walls of a wooden cabin aren't going to do much," I pointed out.

The huge muscle-bound man didn't take his eyes off me, but he did hammer a fist against the front door's wooden frame. Suddenly the entire cabin ignited for a brief second with bright orange light, and in that light I saw strange magical patterns that burned a brighter shade of orange.

"You're a wizard?" I asked.

"No, but I've got friends in the right places. This cabin is protected, you'll be safe here. Now get inside. You can keep the wand pointed at me if it makes you feel better."

I looked down, not even realizing I had the wand pointed at him. "I... might just do that. Okay. You have five minutes to explain yourself, but don't get too close."

I walked slowly past the behemoth man, my guard up with every passing step. I entered the cabin and found myself in a large open-plan room consisting of a living room and kitchen. A dying fire was crackling away in a stone hearth on the far left wall. The scent of pine and earth was heavy on the air, along with a comforting scent of masculine musk. As I looked around the room I noticed a lot of cardboard boxes, and not much in the way of personal possessions.

"You just moved here?" I asked as the stranger closed the door behind me and came into the cabin.

"Just transferred," he confirmed with a nod of his head. "Do you want a coffee?"

"Sure," I said. It meant I wouldn't be getting back to sleep now, but I figured the chances of that happening were slim anyway.

"It's Zora, right?" he said as he made his way into the kitchen and turned the kettle on.

"You know everything else about me, I'm guessing you already know my name."

"You're correct." He turned around and pulled two cups out from a cupboard on the kitchen wall. As he did so I noticed just how broad he was, his back a rippling expanse of muscle. He turned around and set the cups down on the counter. "I figured another introduction was necessary. I gave you my name back there, but it's easy to forget details in intense situations. I'm Blake, Blake Voss."

"So, who are you, Blake Voss, and why do you seem to know everything about me? And why are you following me?"

"I already told you, I've been assigned to look after you. I'm your keeper."

"Right. Assigned by who exactly?"

"My pack. We have a long existing pact with your kind."

"My *kind?*" I asked. I was also wondering about the word *pack*, but I had to take this one question at a time.

"Witch-kin. I'm a shifter. I'm part of the Voss pack, well, I'm the leader actually."

"I'm sorry, shifter, pack?"

"Werewolves," Blake said as if it was the plainest thing in the world. "You mean to tell me you've never heard of werewolves before?"

"I've been a witch for like a month," I said. "I had no ideas werewolves were even a real thing."

"Well… now you know, and now you know about the pact. That's why I was following you. I got here a few days ago and I've been scoping out the scenery during that time."

I stared at Blake. By all accounts he was a beautiful man—tall, dark, handsome—but there was something a little unnerving about the idea that he'd been following me. "How long is this arrangement supposed to last exactly?" I asked him.

"How old are you?" he asked.

"Twenty-five. What does that have to do with anything?" I said.

"If you live to eighty then we're looking at fifty-five years," Blake said plainly.

"Fifty-five years of what?"

"Me protecting you."

I opened my eyes wide and shook my head slightly. "I'm sorry, are you suggesting you're going to be following me around for the rest of my life?"

"Yes, or until I die. Should that happen, you will be assigned a replacement keeper."

I blinked, staring at the man that I now *knew* to be crazy. "I think I'm going to decline, but thanks. And that's not to disrespect you saving me back there. I am grateful for that, really."

"I'm afraid it doesn't really work that way," Blake said with an irritating smirk. "Don't worry, most of the time I'll be in the background. As we get to know one another better I can further my distance too."

"I'm just a little confused why *I* need this," I said. "Does every witch have their own werewolf guardian?"

Blake laughed as though the idea was ridiculous. "No, but a long time ago the witches in this valley saved my pack's ancestors from ruin. They swore an oath to always protect an arch witch in Compass Cove."

"Arch witch?" I asked.

Blake blinked at me. "Man, they really didn't tell you anything, huh?"

Just then a knock came at the door. I jumped with a start, but Blake barely reacted. "It's them," I said.

He shook his head. "No, they can't touch the magic boundaries on this cabin."

"But who else knows we're here?" I asked.

Blake walked over to the door and opened it. Although he seemed calm, I was ready for more trouble. I had my fingertips ready to grab my wand, and when Blake opened the door I eased off. Standing there was my grandmother, Liza Wick.

A BRUNCH WITH DEATH

"Liza?" I said in confusion. "What are you doing here?"

"Clearing some things up," she said as she stepped inside, looking at the cabin with dissatisfaction in her eyes. "Go and check the town," she said to Blake. "I'll take care of this."

Blake nodded and looked back at me. "Be seeing you around, Zora."

With that Blake took off, leaving me alone with my grandmother, the woman that was responsible for bringing me here in the first place. "Sit down, Zora, there are some things you need to know."

CHAPTER 7

"*A*pple strudel?" Liza asked, summoning a bowl of the pastries with a snap of her fingers.

"Why the hell not," I said, reaching forward to grab one. We were sitting opposite from one another on the old sagging couches in the cabin. A dusty coffee table stood between us. Liza was sitting in her prim and proper way, looking like she'd rather be anywhere else than this old wooden shack.

She took a sip of coffee that she had poured for herself and made a face, quickly setting the cup back down on the table and pushing it away. "Ugh, werewolves. They can do a lot of things but make a good cup of coffee they cannot."

I took a sip of my own, which I had neglected up until this point. Liza could be unnecessarily snobby at times, so I thought she was just overreacting, but after tasting the brew I found myself making the same face and pushing the cup away. "Wow, that is… a flavor alright."

"I expect you have some questions," Liza said. "I have some too. You may go first."

"Um, okay. Where do I start. Ah, yes, why is a supermodel were-wolf stalking me?"

"Easy on the eyes, isn't he?" Liza said with a delighted grin. "Blake's family are very old friends of our family, Zora. Many generations ago our ancestors saved their ancestors, so they made a pact to always protect the arch witch in Compass Cove."

"What's an arch witch?"

"Well, you are," Liza said simply. "An arch witch is simply the most powerful witch in an area."

"But I've barely been a witch for a month," I said, feeling like I was pointing that out to everyone at the moment.

"Very true, but you *are* a Prismatic Witch, Zora. There are currently only two other known Prismatic Witches in the world, and they are amongst the most powerful. You have magic to learn, but it's only a matter of time."

"But who was the arch witch before me?" I asked. "Don't they need protecting?"

"I was, or should I say—I *am* the current arch witch of Compass Cove. I guess the title will remain with me in an active capacity until you have finished your training."

"So, I've taken away your werewolf guardian?" I asked.

"Hm? No. I have my own keeper, Geraldo, Blake's father. He will remain as my keeper until one of us dies. Truth told he's never had to do much; these days the pact is very much just a ceremonial thing, but that all changes with you."

"Me?"

"Yes, you. Although I'm the arch witch for this area, Zora, my powers aren't far and above the rest of the general witching population. You, however, are a different story. It won't be long until news of your powers grow, and before long every magical faction under the sun will come asking for something. Some will be allies, some will be enemies—make one thing clear, they will all want your power in some way. That is why I preemptively assigned Blake as your keeper, before you officially become the arch witch of Compass Cove. I knew you would need protecting before then."

"So I'm being stalked by this werewolf dude because you put him up to the task?"

Liza thought about the question before nodding. "Yes, that's about the long and short of it. Now, it's my turn to ask questions. I need to you tell me everything that happened tonight."

"Should I start with dinner or get straight to the good stuff?" I joked. Liza rolled her eyes and tapped her fingers over her thighs. "Not in the mood for jokes?"

"Zora, my dear, you could have died tonight. I'm not sure if you realize the gravity of this situation."

"I'm alive, aren't I? What's wrong with using a little humor to lighten the mood?" Liza did crack a smile, but it was definitely forced. "You don't like people much, do you?" I asked her.

"I like them just fine; they just don't make a whole lot of sense to me," she said honestly. I found myself believing her. Liza could come across as cold and indifferent at the best of times, but she didn't seem to harbor any genuine ill will towards people. I suspected she had some undiagnosed social developmental disorder.

"Okay," I said. "I went to sleep, and then I got a call in the middle of the night. It was about two in the morning; it was Sabrina. She said she was picking up some stock from a self-storage outside of town and her car had broken down. She needed a ride. I drove to the address she texted me, and found an old, abandoned gas station. I got out of the van and then I saw them standing behind me; five witches in hooded cloaks."

"Did they give you any names? What did they want?" Liza asked keenly.

"They said they were the 'Sisters of the Shade'. The head witch called herself *Morgantha.*"

Liza closed her eyes upon hearing the name, looking like she wished she hadn't heard it. "That old rat, is she still scurrying around?"

"You know her?" I asked.

"I do. We went to school together, many moons ago, though she was a few years above me. She was a cretin, even back then."

"But she looked the same age as me, younger even!" I said.

"The Sisters of the Shade are a group of dark witches that borrow their power from a powerful entity. In return for their servitude, each of them is given a magical gift by the dark power they worship. Morgantha was given the gift of eternal life."

I opened my eyes wide. "Quite the gift!"

Liza pursed her lips. "Do not be tempted, Zora. They pay for their gifts in other ways. I'm guessing then that Morgantha lured you out there to try and recruit you?"

"Yes, and I didn't like their vibe from the get-go. I told them as much, but maybe my language was a little more colorful."

A rare smirk came over Liza's face. "Atta girl. Well, I must say I am proud. You saw them for what they are, and you sidestepped it nicely. Don't be surprised if they return; I doubt it's the last we'll see of them. Good thing Blake was there to save you, though from what he tells me you handled yourself nicely as well, blasting them away with your wand. We'll have to start fast-tracking your training, so you can defend yourself properly next time.

"Next time? This will happen again?" I asked.

"Oh yes," she said calmly. "The Sisters of the Shade have always been a nuisance. They use dark magic to take what they want. The only thing standing in their way are good witches like you and me. We have to hold the line and keep them back in the shadows. Fear not though, as long as you're in Compass Cove you're safe. There are protective magical boundaries around the town that stop dark witches from getting inside, just like this cabin."

"So that's why they lured me out into the wilderness? One of them could make her voice sound like other people. She imitated Sabrina."

"Yes, they are clever and cunning, but you will learn their ways. They cannot enter the town but they *can* manipulate humans into doing their bidding. That's why Blake has gone to check over the apartment before you return, just to make sure it's safe."

"Why do I feel like I have to have my wits about me for the rest of my life?" I asked.

"Because you do, but fear not, you have Blake watching your back now as well. He comes from a long line of highly trained warriors. You have none better than him to watch you. Plus, he's easy on the eyes too, just like his father!"

"Liza!" I said, finding myself amused and mortified as my grand-mother came out of her shell a little. It was a rare thing, but always nice to see.

"What? I was young too once. Anyway, look at the time, I'll have to go. Blake says the apartment is fine."

"He does? But how—"

As Liza stood up, she snapped her fingers. The front door flew open and I saw Blake standing there, just about to come through the doorway. "You're all good to go home," he said to me. "Hop on the chopper. Let's get you back."

I turned around to look at Liza, but she had vanished. "The women in my family…" I muttered to myself. After a quick ride on Blake's chopper, we arrived back at Zelda's apartment. It was still nighttime, but the distant horizon was beginning to brighten with the amber of dawn. A lengthy yawn escaped me as I climbed off the bike.

"Today is going to be rough," I said.

"I've cleared this block and the perimeter, nothing suspicious to me. Try and get some sleep, you'll need it." Blake then let his serious edge ease off a little and lightened up. "If today is as busy as yesterday then it's going to be a hard one for you!"

I stared at him for a moment, blinking as I tried to keep my eyes open. "Can you try and pretend like you haven't been following me everywhere? It's a little weird you knowing so much about me, even if it is apparently necessary."

Blake nodded. "Got it, can do."

"What do you do now, go back to that cabin?"

"At some point. I'm going to stay in the area for a while just to make sure things are safe. You can rest easy, Zora Wick. I've got your back."

"Don't you need sleep? And how have I failed to notice you following me over the last few days? You don't exactly blend in." Not only was Blake taller and larger than most other people in Compass Cove, he looked like he should be on billboards selling swimwear for men—he was hard to miss.

"A few days? I've been guarding you for two weeks now. Let's just say I'm good at my job."

"Do they teach a lot of covert surveillance out in the woods? Is there a werewolf spy school or something that I don't know about?"

Blake smirked. "No, most of what I know I learned as a Green Beret."

"If I had a drink, I would spit it in your face right about now. You were a Green Beret?"

"Technically it's a title for life, but yes, I served."

"Remind me to never piss you off. Anyway, I better turn in and try and get an hour or two before I have to wake up. I'll... see you around?"

"Indeed. If tonight has shaken you then I don't want you to worry. I've got your back, Zora."

With that, Blake turned the throttle and his bike pulled off down the street. He turned at the end of the block and then he was gone.

* * *

"Go over it again, but very slowly—" Zelda said the following morning as we ate breakfast at her kitchen table.

"They called themselves the Sisters of the Shade—" I began.

"No, no," she interrupted. "The werewolf bodyguard! I want details. How tall was he? What color were his eyes? Do you have an estimate on his chest and bicep measurements?"

I stared at my sister, and I noticed Hermes and Phoebe—who had both joined us in the kitchen—were staring at her too. Zelda noticed the attention. "What?! I'm just trying to paint a mental picture in my mind, so I have the story straight!"

"It's funny how you didn't ask for Morgantha's bicep measurements though," Hermes pointed out.

"Anyway, it was one heck of a night, and I feel like the dead. I probably got about two hours sleep after Blake dropped me off here."

"I don't like the idea of dark witches lurking around, especially folks like the Sisters of the Shade; they're bad news," Hermes said.

"What do they do exactly?" I asked. "Do they hurt people?"

"Like kill? No, they're not *that* bad, but they aren't pleasant either. Dark magic feeds off dark energy. Paranoia, anxiety, depression, that's their bread and butter. They drain humans and take their energy to make themselves stronger," Hermes explained.

"They sound like a pleasant bunch," I muttered, taking another bite of my marmalade on toast.

"And what use were you?" Hermes said, turning his attention on Phoebe. "Your witch gets kidnapped, and you couldn't even give her a warning? For someone that can see into the future—"

"Can't see the future, just a broader slice of the present," Phoebe corrected. "Besides as an Olaphax I'm bound by the laws of time. I can't report meaningful things that haven't happened yet, bad or good."

"So, you *are* just a talking weather station," Hermes harumphed.

"Can we get through breakfast without having an all-out familiar wrestling match?" I asked.

"Yeah," Zelda agreed. "My kitchen isn't big enough. Besides, Phoebe would wipe the floor with you, Hermes."

"I beg your pardon!" Hermes said with indignation. "That feathered rat? I could take her!"

"Did you know that owls kill some prey by flying up high and dropping them?" Phoebe asked, in a voice that was chillingly calm. "Even some prey as large as a housecat."

Hermes looked spooked. "But you're not an owl. You're an Olaphax!"

"Then I guess today is your lucky day," Phoebe said. Zelda and I both bit back our smirks and took a long sip of our coffees.

"Well, I better hit the road. Celeste has got this date, sorry, I mean —'foot doctor' thing—and I've got to take care of the café by myself." Zelda looked at me. "Put an ad in the paper. You need to hire an assistant."

"Don't most people look for jobs online now?" I asked.

"Most mortals maybe. I'm talking about the magic paper. Get with the times, grandma."

"I'll make a note to do that," I grumbled.

"I'll put a message in the group chat to let Sabrina and Celeste know about last night. If you're in danger, then we're all potentially in danger. Are you sure you're okay on your own today?" Zelda asked.

"I'm fine. Apparently this Blake guy is always stalking around anyway. He said he's got my back."

Just then someone started hammering at Zelda's apartment door. We both jumped and looked at one another. "Expecting someone?" I asked her.

"It's them!" Hermes panicked. "The dark witches have come to kill us!"

"Police! Open up!" the voice came through the door.

"Police?" I said, looking at Zelda. "What did you do?"

"What did I do?!" she squeaked. "I didn't do anything!"

"This *is* your apartment," I said.

"Let's just get this over with," Zelda said, marching towards the door. Before she opened it, I pulled her back and stopped her.

"Wait. What if this is another trap? What if it's the Sisters of the Shade?"

Zelda yanked her arm out my grasp and peered through the peep-hole. "It's Burt and his two sons. Let's just open up and see what they want." With that Zelda opened the door. Sure enough there was Burt Combs and his two sons, three of the four members of Compass Cove's sleepy police force.

"Zora Wick I'm going to have to ask you to come down to the station. We've got some questions."

"If this is about my van I'm going to get it now—"

"Do you recognize this man?" Burt said, holding up a photo of a smooth-faced man with white hair.

"Hey, I do recognize him. He was in my bakery yesterday. Quite the jerk actually, can't remember his name though—"

"Mark Mobson." Burt looked back into the corridor. "Voss, come in here and walk her out."

Wait a second, Voss?

Just then another officer came into view, a mountain of a man with bulging muscles and dark brown eyes that seemed to pierce right through me. "You!" I said, gasping as Blake came into Zelda's apartment. He circled behind me and started walking me out.

"What's going on here?!" Zelda shouted at Burt.

"Mark Mobson dropped dead yesterday afternoon. The autopsy found poison in his system, traced back to a brownie that he purchased at your bakery—we have it all on video."

"But, but!" I protested as Blake marched me out of the apartment.

It didn't look like I'd be selling much today.

CHAPTER 8

"In here," Blake said, guiding me into an interview room at the police station and sitting me down at a metal table. He was wearing a full police officer uniform, acting as though he'd been at the station his entire life. At the moment it was just the two of us.

"What happened to you having my back?" I hissed, trying not to stare at him. He looked irritatingly good in his cop uniform.

"I do have your back," he said calmly. "But I also have to do my job."

"The least you could do is uncuff me!" I said. "I didn't kill that guy!"

"Sure looks like you did," Blake said, that irritating smirk lifting on his perfect lips once again.

I just scowled at him in disbelief and shook my head. "Just wait until Liza hears about this."

Blake laughed. "You think I report to Liza?"

"I don't care who you report to. I didn't kill that guy," I repeated.

Blake rolled his eyes and blinked slowly. "Look, I believe you, but I still have to do my job."

"And since when do you work for the police station?"

"Since last week," Blake said. "You're looking at Compass Cove's newest recruit."

"What happened to the whole Green Beret werewolf guardian thing, or was that just all a lie?"

Blake glanced around the empty room, his eyes flitting to the mirror on the wall. "Keep it down, alright? You don't see me airing all your magical laundry in here. That stuff is all still true. I got this job so I could be close to you."

The door to the interview room opened and Sheriff Burt came in, with a laptop and some paperwork slowly sliding out of his arms. "Ah, Zora, did I introduce you to Voss? He's our newest recruit at the station. Guy looks like an action hero, doesn't he?!"

"Looks more like a clown to me," I muttered.

"That'll be all for now, Blake, thanks. Have Linda bring in some coffee, will you? You can get back to the street."

"Will do, sir." Blake left the room with a dutiful nod, winking at me as he did so.

"So, Zora Wick..." Burt said as he shuffled paperwork about and opened up the laptop. He took a seat at the table and smiled at me. "How are things?"

"They've been better, Burt," I said, holding up my cuffed hands. Burt looked at them as though he'd forgotten I was cuffed in the first place.

"Ah, let me get them off for you," he said, reaching over the table and undoing the cuffs. I rubbed at my wrists and thanked him begrudgingly.

"Thanks. Care to tell me what's going on here?"

"Once the joe gets here, yes. I don't do any interrogation without my morning java. Ah, here she is!" Burt said warmly as his wife, Linda, came into the room with two cups of coffee. She set them down, pulled her police badge off her shirt and examined it closely.

"Huh, that's funny," she said.

"What's that?" Burt asked her.

"Well on this badge it says 'To Protect and Serve'. It doesn't mention anything about me being a waitress!" Linda gave Burt a playful slap on the side of his head, he laughed and gave her an affectionate squeeze around the waist. "You're just the person I wanted to see," Linda said to me as she pulled a small puzzle book out of her rear pocket.

"Seriously?" I said. "You're hitting me up for crossword puzzle clues now? I'm being interrogated for murder!"

"Four down," Linda said, ignoring me as I protested her inappropriate manner. "Food with an edible shell."

"Snail?" Burt hazarded. "The French eat snails, don't they?"

"They don't eat the shells, you dummy!" Linda scoffed. She looked at me. "Come on, this one's had me stumped all of yesterday. I thought maybe it was mussels, but you don't eat the shell on them either…"

"Maybe some sort of lobster?" Burt guessed.

"It's taco," I said with a regretful sigh.

"Taco!" Linda said, her face lighting up with joy. She pulled her pen out and inked in the answer. "What did I tell you, Burt? This girl would have the answer, she's a treasure! We need to have her on the books as a full-time consultant. After all this is sorted of course," she said, waving her pen at the interview table and corresponding room. "Go easy on her, Burt dear; that one kept me up last night."

Linda left the interview room, chuckling and singing to herself as she did so. Burt pushed a coffee across the table to me and turned his attention back to the open laptop. "So, Mark Mobson," he said, mostly speaking to himself.

"You can't seriously think I killed that guy," I said.

"I'm of two minds, Miss Wick," Burt said. "On the one hand you just helped us solve your aunt's murder, but on the other hand…" Burt turned the laptop around and hit the space bar, leaning back as he let a video play. Straightaway I could tell it was the streaming footage from Mark Mobson's phone.

"And what do we have here?" Mark said as he walked down the street that my bakery was on. "A bakery, open at this hour? Alright, chat. Let's take a vote. Should I go into that miserable little shop or not?"

For the next five minutes I had to sit there and watch as I relived my unfortunate run-in with the miserable Mark Mobson. I had to admit that I didn't come across particularly well in the video, Mark was good at pushing buttons it seemed. Mind you, he didn't come across well either.

The video ended when Mark left the shop, featuring a little conversation I hadn't been privy to on the day. "Ooh, well wasn't she a feisty one? I think I'll come back and get her number anyway; she definitely seemed interested. I'm not eating the brownie now, guys, it feels molten hot. I'll put it in my pocket and have it later. Right, let's go down to the gym and see if we can find any hot girls to chat up!"

I took a deep breath as the video came to an end. "Why am I watching this again?" I asked Burt.

"Evidence," he said, taking a bite of a donut that he had produced from... somewhere. "Your run-in with Mark Mobson doesn't exactly look good. Tell me, why did you go into the back of the bakery to get him a brownie slice?"

"Because that's what he asked for?" I said. "I was going to get him one from the cabinet. You heard that guy, he was giving me a hard time!" I then sat up straight as something occurred to me. "Hang on a second. I shouldn't be talking to you without a lawyer."

Burt lifted a querying brow. "That's entirely within your prerogative. Do you want to call your lawyer?"

"I... I don't have one," I said as it dawned upon me.

"I can call you a public defender?" Burt offered.

"Yes, but until then... my lips are sealed! I can do that... right?"

Burt nodded genially. "Absolutely. I kind of expected you might. Sit tight. I'll see who I can dig up."

Twenty minutes later the door of the interview room opened again and a disheveled looking man in an ill-fitting brown suit rushed inside, a briefcase in one hand, a coffee flask in the other. "Zena Wax!" he said, his voice nasal with a strong New Jersey accent. "What did you do this time, ye rascal?" He rolled his eyes and looked at Burt, who was standing in the doorway. "Give me a minute alone with my client please, Sheriff. Ol' Kenny has work to do!"

"Five minutes," Burt said as he shut the door.

"Do I know you?" I said to the man in the brown suit, puzzled by his overfamiliarity.

"Kenny King! Public defender to the stars!" Kenny said, holding his hand out to shake mine. As he did so his briefcase fell open, bags of gummy bears spilling out onto the floor.

"Are those... gummy bears?" I asked. Kenny pulled his hand away and dropped to all fours, quickly scooping up the bags of candy back into his briefcase. He snapped the case shut again and stood up, a slight sweat breaking out on his brow.

"I don't know you," I said, mostly stating it for my own benefit.

"No, but soon we'll be best friends."

"Why act like you know me then?" I asked. "When you came in here you were acting very familiar."

"Oldest trick in the book, Miss Wax. Always keep the police guessing, never give them any clues! You either die young or go out in a blazing battle of gunfire. Well, let me tell you one thing for free; those pigs will never take me alive! Am I making sense here?"

"Not one bit. Now, about those gummy bears—"

"So, Zena—" he began, ignoring my question.

"It's Zora. Zora Wick," I corrected.

Kenny pulled a handwritten note from his blazer pocket and stared closely at it. "Man, I really gotta improve my handwriting!" Kenny threw himself down in a chair and started looking through a file. "So Zora, you killed a guy with a poison brownie." Kenny slammed the folder shut, looked up at me, and brushed a hand back through his balding and somewhat greasy hair. "I'll be straight with you here. We're looking at twenty, but with a confession and good behavior you could be out in five!"

"I didn't kill the guy!" I said in disbelief.

"Oh, oh of course!" Kenny said, sitting back in his chair and smoothing out the lapels on his creased suit. He winked at me very deliberately. "I mean who knows who would be listening. Obviously you didn't kill Miss—"

"Mister," I corrected.

Kenny quickly opened the file and shut it again. "Mister Mark Mobson. *Obviously*, you didn't kill that guy, but let's say you did—"

"I didn't," I said, crossing my arms over one another. "I think I'm going to get a different lawyer."

"Zena, Zena!" Kenny said, jumping up to his feet quickly and throwing his hands out to steady the waters. "Give me a chance, I'm 25-3 and I work hard! I know I might not look like a superstar attorney, but I promise you, you can't go wrong with Kenny King!"

"My name is Zora," I said, sighing to myself and pushing my fingers into the bridge of my nose.

"Right, right. That's what I said. Listen, if you say you're innocent then you are innocent! I'm going to need to know everything about you and the victim, your relationship, your ups, your downs, his sexual preferences—"

"Let me stop you right there, Kenny. I barely knew the guy. He came into my bakery, ordered a brownie, ate it, and dropped dead later that day. That's the whole kit and caboodle. They got the whole interaction on video; he was a streamer."

"Streamer? A fisherman, eh. Well, I don't know what that has to do with it, but I fish myself—well, my old man did at least. Listen, Zena—"

"Zora."

"Listen, *Zora*, doll, with a face like yours we could be in for some trouble here. Juries like to send pretty girls like you to the chair!" Kenny once again flapped through the paperwork, like a kid trying to cram last-minute before a test. "It says here the autopsy found 'strikneen' in his system, sourced to the brownie he purchased from your bakery."

"It's pronounced *strychnine*," I said. "It's a very famous poison, in a lot of old mystery books."

Kenny laughed nervously and looked over at the giant mirror to our right. "Haha! Good one, Zora!" He leaned in close to me and lowered his voice. "Ixnay on the poison-nay."

"I'm fairly sure most people know about strychnine," I said.

"I don't know poison, Zora, I know the law, and I know one thing for sure. This case does *not* look good for you. Like I said, you've got a face that could sell church pews—" What the heck did that mean? "A jury will take one look at you and flip the switch."

"I'm almost certain they don't have the death sentence in this state."

Kenny stared at me for a moment as though trying to call up that lost piece of information in his mind. "Yeah... yeah you're right, of course. I was speaking figuratively."

I groaned once again. "How are you up twenty-five cases against three?"

"What? No, I *lost* twenty-five cases. I won three, and that's technically because they were thrown out on technicalities. Heck, the judge died of a heart attack in one of them."

"Are you kidding me?" How on earth did I land an attorney *this* bad?

"No, the judge was a big guy and apparently he liked his red meat—"

"I'm doomed," I said, sitting forward and dropping my head into my hands.

"Listen, Zara. My good luck streak is just around the corner; that's what Ma says at least anyway."

"Yeah, I think I'm definitely going with another lawyer."

"Tell you what, out of the goodness of my heart I'll do this pro bono—"

"You're a public defender—"

"*And* I'll thrown in this coupon for a free car detail too!" he said, fishing a crumpled-up coupon out of his pocket and putting it on the table.

"This expired two years ago," I said, reading the coupon.

Kenny jumped up, gathered his things and banged on the door. Sheriff Burt opened it a moment later. "Alright, Chief, we're ready to—"

"It's your lucky day, Wick," Burt said as he came into the room. "Someone posted your bail. You're free to go."

"What, who?" I said in confusion. Just then, he stepped into the doorway, my heart catching in my throat as soon as I set eyes on him. "Hudson?!"

Hudson nodded at me. "Grab your things, Wick. We're getting out of here."

CHAPTER 9

"So... where have you been?" I said as we drove away in Hudson's car. "What happened to your bike?"

"The bike was just a part of the undercover image," Hudson said with a smile. "I thought you would have figured out by now that I'm not actually an outlaw biker. I'm an undercover agent."

"Right, right, and you hand out business cards that self-immolate, for some reason." The last time I'd seen Hudson he'd handed me a business card that set itself alight a few seconds later. "Seems a bit pointless if you ask me."

"MAGE are quite secretive, but they have to be. Can't have the general public knowing about magic. Can you imagine the chaos that would cause?"

I briefly considered the idea, and yes, chaos was probably an apt description. "But you're not magic, are you?" My fingertips weren't crackling, so it meant Hudson wasn't magical, but I did feel an odd aura around him, and my heartbeat was probably twenty beats a minute higher ever since he'd walked into the interrogation room.

"Um, no, I'm not, but—"

"But what?" I asked, keen to see where this was going.

"Let's just say working at MAGE has opened up some doors for me," Hudson said.

"Right. Whatever that means. So where have you been? You saved my sister's life and then you disappeared into thin air."

"It's called having a job," Hudson said. "Compass Cove is my primary area, but right after the business with Slade I got pulled out of the area for another job. That's the thing about this business; it can take you anywhere."

"And what is your business? You're an agent, I know that much, but what do you do?"

"I put right things that are wrong, make sure normal people don't get hurt, and if I get time, I post bail for beautiful girls that talk too much."

Did he just say beautiful? "You know it's the twenty-first century. Misogyny doesn't really fly anymore."

"Hey, I'm as progressive as the next guy, just giving you a hard time, relax. I thought you'd be a little happier to see me, since I just got you out of jail and all."

"I am, thanks. I'll pay you back when I get the money. Business is a little tight at the moment, I've been shut down for—" I paused, about to stop myself from telling Hudson about the Poxy infestation. "Wait, I can talk to you about magic stuff, right?"

Hudson nodded. "I've got clearance through my position at MAGE. Talk away, Wick. What's up with the bakery?"

"I've got a Poxy infestation, and apparently they're the bad kind."

Hudson made a face as though he only knew all too well. "Ooh, Poxy. Yeah those things can be a real pain in the butt. Make sure you get an exterminator that will go full scorched-earth; you don't want Poxy coming back."

"I… kind of asked for nonlethal extraction."

Hudson just laughed. "Of course you did."

"So, you're back in the area now?" I asked.

"As of this moment, yes. My other job is finished, so I can focus on Compass Cove again."

"What was the other job?"

"Rogue boogeyman, causing a lot of trouble in a place called Pendle Island. Nice place, quite the ride from here. Locals are mad as a box of frogs though."

"Boogeyman?" I asked. "You're telling me the boogeyman is actually real?"

"Yes, they manifest when areas of negative energy build up. Usually when a concentrated area of magic folk start having bad dreams. Typically, they show up around the end of the tax year."

I laughed. "Ha, I wonder why. So what do these boogeymen do?"

"Boogeyman," he corrected. "Most of the time there's just one. Once they get strong enough, they can manifest themselves physically, but only at nighttime. That's when the trouble starts. They look like a person but made of shadow. They run around causing trouble. Slapping people awake, pinching people, sometimes they take kids too."

"That escalated quickly!" I said. "Did that happen?"

"No, but there are historical reports of them eating people if left unchecked for long enough. This one was a real pain in the butt too. I was chasing him all over town for four nights. He got a couple of good hits in."

"And how does a regular human like you capture a magical entity like that?" I asked.

Hudson looked at me and winked. "Who said anything about me was regular?"

I rolled my eyes. Hudson clearly liked the enigmatic image he projected.

"So, where are you taking me?" I asked, wondering where we were driving exactly.

"I thought we'd grab a bite to eat, if that's okay with you. We never got that date sorted."

My heart started galloping in my chest. "Date?" I said, my voice catching in my throat.

"Yeah…" Hudson said, looking over at me and smiling in an amused way. "Is that okay? Or did you start seeing someone since I was gone?"

"Um, no, it's just… I haven't really done my hair, and I didn't sleep much last night, and I'm supposed to be working too—the van!"

"Van?" Hudson asked, wondering what the alarm was about.

"It's a long story," I said. "Could you help me out with something?"

"That depends. What's the story?"

I then recounted the night's events to Hudson, starting with the spoof phone call from the dark witches, all the way up to Blake showing up and saving me. Halfway through the story Hudson started driving in the direction of the old gas station, agreeing to pick up my car. I finished recapping the events just as we reached the town's north border.

"And this werewolf, what did he look like?" Hudson asked.

I was about to open my mouth to answer when a huge figure suddenly crashed down onto the road about twenty feet in front of us. Hudson brought the car to a screeching halt, threw one hand across my chest, and with is other hand he pulled out a pistol.

"What now?" Hudson hissed under his teeth. He opened the car door to get out when I stopped him.

"No, wait! That's him!"

"Who?" he asked in confusion, looking up the road at the policeman that had now stood up straight.

"Him! That's Blake. My werewolf guy!"

I expected that alone would be enough to put Hudson at ease. Instead he snarled and kicked his driver door open. "Stay here," he ordered. "Let's see what this moron wants."

I closed my eyes and sighed, realizing what was about to go down.

"Oh goody," I grumbled to myself, unclasping my seatbelt to get out and chase after Hudson. "Two alpha male idiots are about to butt heads."

* * *

"JUST WHAT THE hell do you think you're doing, falling out of the sky like that?" Hudson said, stopping short of Blake by a few feet. Blake had also marched forward, stopping at the same time as Hudson.

"Stopping you from making a big mistake," Blake growled back. "Just who are you, anyway?"

At this point I caught up to them both. "Blake, this is Hudson. He helped me out with some trouble a few weeks ago. Saved mine and my sister's life. He knows about magic."

Blake turned his head at hearing Hudson had saved my life. "If you saved Zora's life you can't be a complete idiot, but she can't go outside the town boundary right now. The wrong people are after her."

"I know, she told me," Hudson said through clenched teeth.

"Then you'll know the safest place for her is inside the boundary. What are you, an idiot?"

"Funny, I was about to ask you the same thing," Hudson snapped.

"Can you both chill?" I said. "What is going on here? Blake, I asked Hudson to help me get the van back. I need to get some work done at some point this week."

"I told you I'd help you with the van," Blake said, his tone easing as he addressed me.

"You, Hudson, what difference does it make?" I asked.

Blake looked back at Hudson, his brow furrowing once again. "The difference is you can trust me; I don't know anything about this guy."

"Ditto," Hudson mirrored. I rolled my eyes.

"You can trust him," I said. "He's with—" I stopped myself before I spilled all of Hudson's magical secrets.

"It's alright, a dog like this can know. I'm with MAGE, and if you must know, they sent me back here to keep an eye on Zora full-time. We can't have a Prismatic Witch getting hurt."

I looked at Hudson with surprise. "Wait, that's why they sent you back here? You didn't tell me that."

"I was about to," Hudson said, his tone also softening as he spoke to me. "But then Dog the Bounty Hunter here drops out of the sky like he's in some cliché superhero movie."

"Careful who you're calling dog, little man. I eat punks like you for breakfast," Blake snarled, stepping forward as he did so. "MAGE? What does that make you? A glorified security guard for some wizards that like to hide in an office block."

Hudson just laughed and also stepped forward. Their chests were now inches apart. "You think you're tough because you howl at the moon and turn into a wolf? I've thrown down with bigger werewolves than you. I'm not some regular joe."

"Look, as much as I want to watch you both rip the clothes off one another, I've got better things to do—" I began, but neither of them was listening to me.

"Let's settle this here and now then," Blake said. "Zora only needs one guy looking after her, and I already filled that position. If you want the job, you'll have to fight me for it. Winner gets the gig; loser gets the hell out of town."

Hudson chuckled again, tucked his gun into the holster, and I breathed a sigh of relief thinking he'd come to his senses. Just then the two of them exploded in a blur of supersonic movement. I don't know which one moved first because it was too fast to see. Next thing I knew Blake and Hudson were zooming through the air in every direction, throwing punches at one another, hurling the other through trees, and generally just causing a big old mess.

"Will you stop?!" I shouted, jumping back as a huge pine tree crashed into the road after Hudson had thrown Blake through it. In retaliation Blake caught Hudson in a counter throw, launched him up into the air, and sent him crashing down into the road, causing a huge crater in the lane that led back into town.

Neither of them seemed intent on listening to me, and there was no way I was physically capable of stopping them. With no other choice I pulled out my wand and felt a pang of magical intuition guide me. The two supercharged machismo men flew past me; I opened my mouth and hollered at the top of my lungs.

"Stop!"

With the word a wall of force blasted across the area, freezing Blake and Hudson in their tracks. They crashed to the ground, momentarily statuesque, two snarling brutes tangled in one another. Their shirts were ripped clean off, their torsos covered in cuts and bruises. I walked over to them, put my wand away, and mentally dissolved the spell.

All of a sudden, they pushed away from one another and scrambled to their feet. After my spell had robbed them of their momentum, they were just sort of lying there in each other's arms. Hilarious for me, embarrassing for them.

"What the hell kind of human are you?" Blake snarled at Hudson. "I ain't ever seen a human move like that!"

"Told you I could hold my own," Hudson smirked.

"Yes, you've both proven that you're *very* tough," I said. "Is that out of your systems now? I have a van to pick up. Judging from that rough and tumble I'd say your powers are fairly matched. Why don't you both just be my guardians? Or neither. At this point, I'm not really fussed."

Blake and Hudson both looked at me then as if I was crazy.

"Hang on a second, Zora. You need a keeper," Blake said.

"Can't believe I'm actually agreeing with this idiot, but he's right. You don't understand the tide that's coming," Hudson said.

"And I'm safe here, dodging falling trees and flying pieces of tarmac? I've been doing just fine walking around without having to worry about two three-hundred-pound men throwing each other around."

The pair of them looked around the scene, realizing the damage they had caused. "Perhaps we got a little out of hand," Hudson admitted.

"Surprise, surprise, pumping a human full of magic leads to problems," Blake said. Suddenly the pair of them were face-to-face again. "Just what are you anyway? Some sort of experiment gone wrong?"

"That's enough," I said, anger evident in my voice this time. "My next spell won't be so friendly. How would the pair of you like to spend the rest of a week as a pair of kittens? That idea is sounding real good right about now."

A look of panic shot across Blake's face. "She can do that?" he said to Hudson.

"I'm not about to push it and find out. Zora's right, our powers are equally matched—"

"I was holding back, human," Blake said.

"So was I, *dog*. Let's just agree that we both stick around. Two heads are probably better than one."

I cleared my throat. "Again, I'm open to the option of you both leaving me alone at this point. I have a business to run. Oh, and I also have to clear my name for murder now as well. I don't need this masculine bravado." Though I was sure Zelda and the girls were going to love hearing all about it.

"Not an option," Blake said.

"Agreed. We both stick around," Hudson said, nodding.

"Then find a way to get a long, or pick a territory, or alternate weekends or something. I don't want any more fighting, is that clear?"

"Crystal," Blake answered.

"Clear," Hudson confirmed.

"Good," I said. "Now can I pick up my van and get on with my day? Last I checked I don't need you both babysitting me every single minute. I'm pretty sure I'll hurl you into a tree myself if that's the case."

"I suppose that's fair," Hudson said. I looked at Blake who also nodded in agreement.

"Good. Now clean up this mess," I said, gesturing to the fallen tree parts scattered across the road. The two men both got to work, picking up the huge pieces of tree like they weighed nothing at all. Once they were done we headed back to Hudson's car, which had escaped the encounter unscathed.

"Blake, go and get yourself a new shirt. Head back to town and do your policeman thing. As Hudson was already taking me out to the van he can escort me."

Blake nodded, but turned to Hudson, a fierce expression coming over his face. "If you let one hair on her head—"

"Yawn, you heard the lady. Back to town, puppy. Don't make me roll up the newspaper now."

Blake gave Hudson a look that could boil water but eased off a little at seeing my own glare. With a monumental leap he pounced up from the road, heading back in the direction of town and out of sight. I looked at Hudson, my arms crossed with disapproval.

"What?!" he laughed, pulling a spare T-shirt from a duffel bag on the back seat of the car. He slipped it on and checked his hair in the car mirror. "He started it!"

"Let's go and get the van. After that I don't want to see you for a week."

Hudson fired up the engine and put his foot on the gas. "Funny, I was just thinking the same thing about Officer Woof."

CHAPTER 10

*T*hankfully we found the van undisturbed, the keys lying in the exact spot in the lot where I had dropped them. I thought the dark witches might have messed with my stuff, but Hudson didn't seem so surprised. He said witches like that had their own ways of getting around and stealing a van would be pointless and only slow them down. He checked the van for trackers and found nothing, so I hopped in, Hudson escorting me with his car as I drove back to Zelda's apartment.

By the time I pulled up it was nearly two in the afternoon, far too late to get any baking or selling done. As I had other chores that needed doing, I decided to dedicate the rest of the day to them and told myself I'd make up for lost time tomorrow. With some help from Hermes, I put an ad in the magical paper, requesting the services of an assistant for the bakery. Once the ad was submitted, I planned my bakes for the morning, ran to the shop, and picked up ingredients I would need. I stocked up the baking van, prepped my work areas, and set an alarm to get up early so I could get a head start with baking.

I was making dinner in the kitchen for Zelda and me when Constance popped her head through the wall, scaring the life out of me once again. Once I was over the shock, I chastised her.

"What do you want?" I grumbled.

"Can't a gal stop by and check in on her favorite niece?" Constance asked innocuously. She floated through the wall and sat on the countertop. "I ran by the bakery today; it looks like the extermination is going well. Did you know that man is a geminus?"

"Bitz and Bosch? Yeah. It was quite the surprise when I first found out. Magical twins sharing a body. Makes me feel like I still have a lot to learn."

"Where have you been today anyway? I was flying all over town looking for the van, I didn't see you anywhere. I figured you'd be back out again seeing as yesterday was such a roaring success."

I recounted the events of the last twenty-four hours to Constance, and halfway through the story a tired looking Zelda shuffled through the door, giving a thumbs-up as she collapsed in a seat at the kitchen table without a word. Once my story was done with Constance the questions came tumbling in.

"I'm sorry, you mean to say they tore the shirts clean off one another?" Constance asked.

"Are they equally jacked?" Zelda asked. "Or is one like way hotter?" She seemed a little more animated now, and we hadn't even eaten yet. I plated up the food and brought it over to the table.

"They're both as stubborn as one another, let's just say that."

"I can't believe this; you literally have two hot dudes fighting over you!" Zelda said. "A man sneezed in my mouth today. In my mouth!"

"I'd much rather have taken your day," I said. "I got arrested for goodness' sake. Thanks for showing up at the station to check everything was okay, by the way," I said to Zelda sarcastically.

The comment caught Zelda off guard. "Wait, you mean that was a real arrest? I thought they were messing around. I thought they were just bringing you in to help them with another case. Why didn't you call me?"

"My one call went to Kenny King, Compass Cove's most useless attorney."

"Gosh, are they still letting that guy practice?" Hermes remarked. "I've read about him in the paper. He's a riot!"

"At the moment he's the one thing keeping me from the inside of a jail cell, well, that and Hudson posting my bail. I need to act fast though and try to clear my name. They say this Mobson guy dropped dead in the street. The autopsy said my brownie had poison in it!"

Constance wrinkled her nose. "Well, that can't be right. You were selling brownies on the street all day from the van. Were they from the same batch?"

"They were!" I said, sitting up with excitement as Constance pointed out the obvious. "Constance, I could kiss you! Plenty of other people ate brownies baked at the shop that day, and no one else got sick! Right?"

Zelda shrugged, a mouthful of meatballs and spaghetti spilling onto her plate. "Beats me," she mumbled.

"No other stiffs," Constance said. "I like to check the local morgue each day and welcome any newbies." I turned my head at her comment.

"You do? Did you see a ghost for this Mobson guy?"

"No," she said with a shake of her head. "But I saw them bring the body in. You know for an older man he had a pretty good body; looks like he had a lot of work done though."

I put my fork down and pushed my plate away. "And that's dinner done."

Zelda pulled my plate towards her without missing a beat. "And more for Zelda!"

"I need to figure out how that slice of brownie became poisoned. I mean, that wasn't a happy accident, right? There's got to be a logical explanation here."

"Maybe you have another personality," Hermes posited. "It came out in a moment of rage, and you dosed one slice."

"I'll show you a moment of rage in a minute," I quipped. Just then my phone started ringing. I took the call. "Hello?"

"Is this Zora Wick?" a robotically scrambled voice said.

"Yes, who's speaking?"

"Someone who can help. Meet me at the multistory parking lot behind the old cinema on Yates Avenue."

83

"Who is this?" I asked.

"Tonight, at ten. Come alone."

The line went dead. I tried calling the number back but just got a busy tone.

"Who was that?" Zelda asked. "One of your lover boys checking in on you?"

"I think that was a lead," I said. "Hurry up and eat your food. We're going out."

"But I just got home!" Zelda groaned.

* * *

I'M NOT sure what we were expecting as we pulled up outside the multistory behind the old cinema. Zelda was skittish, but my intuition wasn't picking up anything suspicious.

"What if it's the Sisters of the Shade?" Zelda said in a panicked hush as we went up the stairwell to the top floor.

"It's not," Constance said, popping her head through the wall. Zelda and I both let out a cry of alarm.

"What are you doing here?" I asked.

"I thought I'd scout ahead and make sure it's safe. Seemed like the sensible thing to do. You have an invisible ghost scout; you should use me more often!"

"Your usefulness is debatable; you spend most of your time daydreaming about Bruce Willis or Patrick Swayze," I pointed out.

"How very dare you," Constance said. "You left out Seal. Anyway, there are two women up there; neither of them magical. I'm pretty sure one of them is Linda Combs."

"Linda Combs, from the police station?" I asked. Why on earth would she arrange a cloak-and-dagger meeting like this?

Zelda and I opened the door to the top floor of the lot. There was only one car up here, and its headlights were shining on the silhouette of a lone figure in a trilby and a long parker coat. We approached the figure and stopped.

"I told you to come alone," the figure said, their voice scrambled, just like on the phone call.

"Who, this?" I said, looking at Zelda. "This is my emotional support sister. I'm here to support her emotionally."

"Very funny, Zora," Zelda said, looking at me with disapproval.

"Good job using my name, *Zelda*," I said back.

"Uh, they already know your name. They said it on the phone!" she pointed out.

"Hm. Good point."

"Are you both finished?" the shadowy silhouette asked. "I haven't got all night."

"Linda, we know it's you. Let's just drop the act already."

"Are you kidding me? Okay, Tamara, cut the lights."

The bright headlights went off, and we could now make out Linda's face. She dropped her hand from her throat; she was holding some sort of microphone. "Cool little gadget, eh?" she asked. "I got it at the dollar store. There's even an option to make your voice sound like an elf."

"Linda, what's going on here? Why are we meeting like this?" I asked.

"Well partly because I've always wanted to. The movies make it seem like such good fun. Plus, Tamara wanted a little subtlety."

"This is subtle?" Zelda asked.

"Who is Tamara?" I asked. "And what did you want to talk about?"

"It's about Mobson. You know, the guy you're accused of poisoning."

"Rings a bell," I said sarcastically.

"Tamara, get out already!" Linda said, turning around and slapping the hood of the car with her hand. A figure climbed out of the driver seat and stepped next to Linda; they were wearing a balaclava. Linda pulled the balaclava off, revealing a timid-looking woman with a head full of wild red curls.

"Linda!" Tamara protested, clearly not wanting her face revealed.

"Oh, cool it already," Linda said. "They're good guys. They're on our side."

"But if we don't get some answers, we *will* dish out knuckle sand-wiches," Zelda said in an awful attempt to be threatening. Both Linda and I looked at her.

"You couldn't punch your way out of a paper bag, Zel," I chuckled.

"Could too!" Zelda protested.

"Listen up. girls. We're on a schedule here," Linda said. She looked at Tamara and nudged her. "Tell her."

Tamara swallowed down her nerves and looked at me. "I'm Tamara, Tamara Banana. I'm the coroner that ran the tests on Mark Mobson."

"Wait a second," I said. "Your name is Tamara Banana. For real?"

Tamara pursed her lips then nodded. "Yes. It's my husband's name."

"Okay…" I said, side-eyeing Zelda. "Just checking we're all on the same page here. So, you're the one that found the strychnine in his system."

"Yes."

"And you're the one that said it came from my brownie."

"Yes. Because it did."

"I mean I sold like fifty other slices of brownie to people that day, and none of them died."

"You could have dropped the strychnine onto that particular slice though, with a pipet," Zelda pointed out. Again, I looked at her.

"Who's side are you on exactly?" I asked in disbelief.

"I'm just saying!" she said.

"It wasn't dropped onto the slice," Linda said.

"The strychnine was in the white chocolate drops *inside* the brownie," Tamara said.

"White chocolate drops?" I narrowed my eyes. "There was no white chocolate in the brownie I made that day."

Tamara and Linda looked at one another. "I told you," Linda said. "She's a good egg, plus she's a mean crossword-solver. Actually, that reminds me. Zora—" Linda began to pull out her crossword puzzle book when I stopped her.

"No, Linda, I'm drawing the line here. Not right now. Tell me what's going on. What's with this sneaking around business?"

"I told Tamara there's no way you did it," Linda said. "As the coroner she can make this all go away for you."

"We've all but proved the brownie wasn't mine. Someone must have switched it," I surmised.

"Exactly, but the question is why," Linda said. "How well do you know Mark Mobson?" she asked me.

"I don't know anything about the guy, other than what I learned on the day. He's arrogant, streams his day-to-day, and he claimed he runs Compass Cove's 'most happening' club."

"Well, he left out a few key tidbits," Tamara said. As she did so I realized she was trembling. "Mobson's older brother used to be a professional football player, he had several Superbowl wins."

"Ooh, who?" I asked. Before they could answer I stopped them. "Actually, scratch that. I just remembered I know literally nothing about football."

"Mark Mobson was a no-one," Linda said. "His brother was the rich and successful one. All of Mark's money came from handouts from his brother. He used that cash to start his club."

"Okay," I said, wondering where this was going.

"Here's the thing. Mobson isn't a very good businessman; his club is a black hole for money. His older brother cut him off a few years ago. It left Mark struggling," Tamara said. "That's when the mob stepped in and gave this guy a hand."

"I feel like I know where this is going. Mobson had mob connections..." I groaned.

"That's not all. He's been in trouble before. A few years ago his business partner died, drowned while he was out boating. The official story is that he was drunk, but get this; the coroner report found no alcohol in his system. Instead he'd been sedated with tranquilizers." Tamara was basically shaking now.

"Are you alright?" I asked her. "You look like you've seen a ghost." Looking over my shoulder I did, in fact, see Constance's ghost floating behind us, pretending she was walking on the ceiling. Only Zelda and I could see her though; neither Linda nor Tamara could.

"The coroner came forth with the real cause of death," Linda said. "The next day *they* were found dead."

"The coroner?" I asked in surprise.

"Yah," Tamara said gravely.

My brows lifted high as realization dawned upon me. "I see... so y'all *know* this wasn't me."

"Correct," Tamara said. "But if this is a mob hit—"

"And let's be clear. This *is* a mob hit," Linda interjected.

"Then they want it to look like the brownie killed him," Tamara said.

"But why frame me?! Who am I to the mob?!"

"No one. But I bet my bottom dollar they had eyes on that stream of Mobson's, and they spotted an opportunity to make a bad problem disappear. You're collateral damage, nothing more."

"And you're telling me we have to roll with this false narrative. Otherwise Tamara's going to wake up with a fresh pair of concrete shoes."

"Please, you have to help me!" Tamara said desperately. She looked like she was about to faint. "I never wanted any of this! I'm a cat momma!"

"Hey, lady, we've all got annoying cats at home," I grumbled and looked at Linda, understanding what was at stake here. "You're really giving me no choice other than to solve this."

"You understand what's at stake then. We have to roll with the brownie story for now, even though we know you're in the clear. I don't want anything bad to happen to Tamara, or me, or you even!"

"Nice of you to slip me in at the end there," I said sarcastically.

"Can't we just do witness protection or something?" Zelda suggested. I nodded; it was a good point.

"The last coroner that got whacked *was* in witness protection," Linda said. "The mob has deep roots around here."

"A sleepy little town like Compass Cove, who would have figured?" I asked.

"They don't cause much trouble, Zora, but when they feel threatened they strike. Can you roll with the narrative until we have more answers?"

"Fine," I said, "but can we keep things under wraps? I don't want my face all over this."

"Why do you think we're meeting like this?" Linda asked. "Complete anonymity. Guaranteed. Your name goes nowhere near this, I promise."

Part of me wanted to believe Linda, but the next morning I woke up to a grim surprise.

CHAPTER 11

"I can't believe this!" I said as I held the latest copy of the *Compass Cove Bugle*. There on the front page was an image of my face, with the accompanying headline: *'Dying in the streets! Local baker arrested on suspicion of murder!'*

"Extra, extra, read all about it!" Hermes wailed from the top of the kitchen fridge. "Local woman poisons businessman!" The edges of the newspaper crumbled in my grasp as I lowered it and scowled at Hermes.

"Zelda, quick, give me a spell that will sharply accelerate a cat through a ceiling."

"Idioto ascendo," she joked.

"Didn't work, that's a shame," I muttered. Hermes closed his mouth and gulped.

"I was just lightening the mood!" he said.

Zelda and I were just about to head out for a day in the van when we found the newspaper outside her apartment door. We'd since retreated inside so I could read it. "Linda promised me complete anonymity. Now my face is all over this!"

"If it's any consolation, this does wonders for your street cred. No one will mess with you now," Hermes offered.

"Yeah, and no one will come within a hundred yards of my bakery either," I pointed out. I pulled my phone from out of my pocket and called Linda's direct number. She answered almost straight away, jumping right into conversation.

"Look, I've *just* seen it. I have no idea how this got out," she said.

"Complete anonymity! You promised me!" I bellowed.

"Well, it looks like that ship has sailed. Look, maybe this is good for us. With the story out there now, the mob won't suspect that we're trying to undermine the false evidence. We know Tamara is safe at least."

"Oh well, as long as Tamara Banana is okay. What about me? I've got a reputation to uphold. I've got a business to run!"

"I know you're angry," Linda said. "I would be too."

"Did you put this out there?" I asked her.

"Zora Wick, I would hope you know me better than that by now! I most certainly did not!"

"Then how did it leak?" I asked. "Who else knows?"

"Honey, I don't know. Burt and the boys wouldn't leak it; they hate the press. The only other people that know are Officer Voss and your attorney. I seriously doubt either of them—"

"Wait a second," I said, catching the name of the story's author under the headline. "This says it was written by Carla King."

"That name means nothing to me," Linda confessed.

"That slack-jawed public defender Burt assigned me yesterday was called Kenny King!"

Linda sighed down the phone. "King? He wouldn't. I mean the guy is a sleazeball but—"

"I'll call you back, Linda," I said, ending the call. I dialed Kenny King's number and he answered.

"Kenny King here, attorney to the stars and—"

"Listen here, you shrew-faced rat!" I said. "Why is my face all over the front page of the *Compass Cove Bugle*, and who is Carla King?!"

"Wax? Zena Wax? Is that you?" he floundered. "Hang on a second, you caught me on the wrong foot here, lemme—argh!" An orchestra of audible chaos fallowed. I'm not sure what happened, but it sounded like Kenny tumbled over, crashed through a small coffee table, fell down a set of stairs, and rolled into a glass cabinet full of bowling balls. "Damn foot bath!" King roared as he scrambled for the phone again. "Wax, Wax, are you still there?"

"It's Zora Wick," I said. "Why am I on the front page of the paper, King?"

"I'm just looking at it now for the first time, Wick. I know what this looks like, but you have to understand—"

"Who is Carla King? Why did you sell me out?!"

"Hey!" Kenny shouted, his tone taking a defensive shift. "Kenny King doesn't sell out his clients, you got that?!" He took a deep breath. "Carla is my sister. That two-faced jackanape must have bugged my phone. She's done it before. She's probably listening to this call right now in fact."

I needed somewhere to put my rage, but it was clear Kenny wasn't the right place. "Well get this straight, Carla King. If I see you in the street, you better run!" With that I jabbed my finger at the 'end call' button and slammed my phone on Zelda's kitchen table.

"So, we're threatening journalists now?" Zelda asked. "Just so we're all on the same page."

I dropped my head into my hands and sighed. "Is this a nightmare? I woke up in a nightmare, right?"

"What do you want to do?" Zelda asked me. "We should still get out in the van right, make hay while the sun is shining."

Right now, I just wanted to crawl back into bed, throw the covers over myself and curse the earth, but Zelda had a point. I had to make up for the bakery being closed, *and* missing a day of sales with the van yesterday.

"I suppose we *should* get out there, but I seriously doubt we'll have the same interest now this disaster is floating around town," I said, shaking the newspaper.

"Hey, you know what they say," Hermes piped up. "There's no such thing as bad publicity."

"I'm almost certain this is the definition of bad publicity, Hermes," Zelda argued.

The cat opened his mouth as though to argue the point, but he conceded almost immediately. "Yeah, I don't think we spin this one, Zora. It does not look good for you."

"Thanks, I needed reminding of that."

Regardless of the bad start to the day, we decided then to head out and to ignore the nonsense being printed in the paper. I updated all the business socials, letting the townsfolk of Compass Cove know the bakery van was back on the road today, stopping at Junction Square first of all.

Except that when we got there, we hardly had any customers at all. Apart from a trickle that had most likely not read the paper that day.

"Let's try the park!" Zelda said with determination. "I think there's a chess tournament there today!"

So, Zelda jumped behind the wheel, and we moved the van over to the park. I pinged our new location on the business page and let out my millionth frustrated sigh of the morning. When we got to the park we did have a slight uptick in customers; there *was* a chess tournament going on but not many of the players came over. After half an hour and three sales we were about to leave when a young man in suspenders and large glasses came over.

"I'll take a danish," he said in a nasal voice. "For what it's worth, I don't think you did it." He didn't actually specify what *it* was, but we all knew what the dead elephant in the room was.

"Thanks, your support means the world," I said sarcastically. "Do I know you?"

"No, but I'm approaching this logically. I saw the video that guy posted when he went into your café. You knew he had an audience, no way you'd mess with his food like that! I mean if you think of it like the Muzio gambit, there could *potentially* be a payoff down the line, but as far as chess openings go that's a risky one, though strong if you know what you're—"

"Here's your danish," I said, thrusting the bagged good into his hands. "I don't know what the heck you're talking about, but you can tell your chess nerd friends I'm doing 20% off for the next twenty minutes."

"Oh, they're all terrified of you," he said, pushing up his glasses and slapping a ten-dollar note down. "They're calling you the Brownie Butcher of Compass Cove."

"Tell them to stick to chess," I mumbled as the young man walked away.

"How about we hit up the hospital again. It's lunch right about now, and it was our busiest spot yesterday!" Zelda said cheerily. I knew she was trying to put on a brave face for my benefit, but it couldn't deter me from the fact that we'd barely sold anything all morning.

"Ooh, a bakery van," a familiar voice said. Turning around I saw Blake standing there in his police uniform. "I'll take one hundred donuts."

"Don't do this," I said to him.

"Do what?" he asked, feigning ignorance.

"I don't need your charity."

Blake laughed. "Uh, I've been watching the van all morning. You are in *desperate* need of charity."

"Don't listen to her!" Zelda said, throwing herself in front of me and laughing in a weirdly shrill way, like a horse catching its tail on a fence post. "One hundred donuts coming up! Do you want help bringing them to your car? You're Blake, right? Zora told me all about you saving her the other night. So brave! I'm Zelda, her younger sister."

Zelda had swathed her hands through her hair a dozen times alone during that desperate introduction. Blake gave me a bemused glance then looked at Zelda.

"That would be great, thanks. Just the donuts though; I'm pretty sure I can carry them by myself."

Again, Zelda prefaced her response with an ungodly laugh. "Yeah, I bet you're really strong!" she said, another strange hee-haw laugh coming out of her mouth. "You could probably choke a swan with those puppies!" She leaned forward and gently punched his bicep.

Blake opened his mouth to respond, but the overwhelming

strangeness of Zelda's comment left him speechless. I put my hands on either side of her shoulders and ferried her away from the register.

"Bag up the donuts. I'll take care of this."

"There she goes again!" Zelda laughed as he walked into the back. "Bossing around her single younger sister!" She lingered in the doorway for a moment, waiting for Blake to laugh. He gave an uncomfortable grin. She slipped through the door, catching her head on the side and carrying on as if nothing had happened.

"She seems... nice," he said. "I might actually have the perfect guy for her."

"You have friends that are blind *and* deaf? I don't need you to set my younger sister up with one of your werewolf friends, and I don't need you to buy one hundred donuts from me."

"Hey, this isn't an act of charity. Burt sent me out to get donuts, and those guys go through donuts like they're going out of fashion. Either you sell them to me, or another baker in Compass Cove does." He held out the cash and I took it reluctantly.

"Okay, thanks. This doesn't get you out of the doghouse for yesterday by the way." I paused, reflecting on my choice of words. "Sorry, I wasn't calling you a dog. That's like an insult for a werewolf, right?" Judging by the way Hudson was throwing the word around yesterday, it sure seemed so.

"Don't worry about it." He smiled. "I actually came by to ask you about last night. What was the meeting in the parking garage about?"

"You know about that?" I asked. "Wait, of course you do. You really are following me everywhere, aren't you?"

"Like I said, it's kind of in the job description. Is everything okay?" I quickly walked Blake through the encounter in the parking garage, from meeting Linda and Tamara to seeing my face in the paper this morning. "So, the mob is involved in this somehow," he said. "Figures. That Mobson guy gives off the vibe."

Zelda came back through the door, carrying Blake's boxed donuts. "Are you sure you don't need a hand with these, Blake?"

"I'm fine, thanks," he said, taking the boxes off Zelda. "They smell great. You did a good job."

Zelda answered with another baffling schoolgirl laugh, twirling a lock of hair in her finger as she wandered into the back of the van. Once again, she bumped into the doorframe on her way.

"Tell you what, I'm going to dig into this a little, see what I can turn up," Blake said.

"The mob thing?" I asked.

He nodded. "It's a potential threat, and it's my job to check them out. I'll have a look around and get back to you once I know more." With that, Blake took his one hundred donuts and disappeared out of sight. I was grateful for his charity—because that's obviously what it was—but even with that generous bump we were still way down on the morning.

After that we decided to take the van to the hospital to try and off-load some goods. I'd already prepared an entire day's worth of stock, and I really didn't want it to go to waste. It was already clear there were going to be leftovers today. As I was near the hospital, I figured I could call it a day after this spot and donate any remaining cakes and goods to the hospice.

"You're assuming they'll take them," Zelda said after I told her my plan. We were parked up in the same spot as the day before. The last time we were here we were moving nonstop because business was booming, but today people were actively steering clear of the van.

Only a smattering of customers came to the van in the hour we were there. The entire time Zelda tried to pass the idle minutes by asking endless questions about Blake.

"Do you think he's more of a horror or a western kind of guy? I bet he likes both. I bet on a first date he'd go for the classic dinner and a movie, but he'd make it feel special, you know?"

I just stared at her. "He's not *that* good-looking. Can't you talk about someone else?"

"Okay, let's shift gears. What about Hudson?"

"What about him?" Hudson asked as he stepped up to the van.

"Ah, I forgot I have two stalkers now," I said.

"I'm not stalking you. I was actually in the area on other business. I saw your van and figured I'd come over. Who's stalking you. That Blake bothering you again?"

"If by bothering you mean buying one hundred donuts," Zelda said.

"Zelda," I said in admonishing tone. I didn't want to tell Hudson about Blake visiting the van; I knew he'd try and one-up him.

"What?!" she remarked.

"He bought one hundred donuts?" Hudson said, shifting his weight defensively. "Why would he do that?"

"Because I'm the town leper," I said. "He said it wasn't an act of charity, but it clearly was."

Hudson looked confused. "Why do I feel like I missed something?"

"Didn't you see the paper?" Zelda asked. "You probably don't have time because you were in the gym or styling your hair." She said it in a dreamy way, staring at Hudson for a few seconds too long. I flicked her on the nose to snap her out of her daydream. "Hey!" she said.

"Go and start boxing things up in the back. We'll drop it off at the hospice and get out of here." Zelda grumbled something about me embarrassing her in front of Hudson before slinking into the back.

"What happened in the paper?" Hudson asked.

"You really haven't seen it?"

"No, I've been running around town all night chasing down an escaped Bunyip."

"What's a Bunyip? It sounds cute."

"Imagine a scaley dog-sized sabretooth tiger that can scream so loud it shatters all the windows in a ten-block radius."

"Okay, not so cute then. Where did that come from?"

"A witch was illegally keeping one as a pet. I caught the thing anyway and it's been evacuated to a magical sanctuary for safe storage. Little bugger managed to rip a chunk out of my side though during the process." Hudson lifted up his T-shirt. The side of his abdomen had two deep claw marks across the flesh.

"Ouch," I remarked. "Are you okay?"

"I'm fine." He grinned. "Occupational hazard. So, what happened in the paper?"

"My face, front page news, headline about me poisoning Mobson."

"Ah," Hudson said. I filled him on the rest too, about the evidence clearing me, but the false narrative we had to peddle so not to draw the ire of the mob.

"Well, I already worked a little alongside the mob during my undercover period here," Hudson said. "I'll look into things, see if I can pull up some tidbits to help you out."

"Blake already said he'd look into it," I remarked.

Hudson pursed his lips. "Well, I'll look into it better. Also, I want two hundred of those cookies," he said, pointing to the closest cookie in the display.

I rolled my eyes. "You don't have to do this."

"Do what? I'm just a guy that likes cookies."

"Have you ever eaten a single carb?" I joked. "You don't strike me as the type."

"I dabble now and then," he said with a grin. "If you must know it's actually for the guys and gals back at the office."

"Right, these mysterious witches and wizards at MAGE. And where is their super-secret headquarters by the way?"

"I can't tell you that, it's super-secret. But I *can* invite you along if you're interested in interviewing. They're very intrigued to meet you."

"It's a tempting offer, but I have a bakery to run into the ground, and I've got to clear my name with this Mobson thing. Zelda, we need two hundred cookies boxed up, stat!"

"On it!" she shouted from the back. A loud clattering sound followed. "I'm okay!"

CHAPTER 12

*a*fter a little small talk Hudson left with the cookies, vowing once again to look into the mob issue for me, *"Much better than that dolt, Blake."* When he was gone, I helped Zelda box up the rest of the unsold goods and we ran them over to the hospice to donate. The girl at the counter looked a little uneasy as I came in, but she did take the donations, nonetheless.

On the drive back to Zelda's apartment my phone started pinging, and as I opened it up, I saw several emails in my inbox.

"Anything fun?" Zelda asked from behind the wheel.

"Potentially. I have a few responses to that ad I put in the paper asking for a baking assistant." I quickly scrolled through the emails, finding myself uninspired by the responses so far.

"That face doesn't look promising," Zelda remarked. "I'm guessing the current applicants fall short?"

"There's a resume here from a witch called 'Verity Soil'. She doesn't have any experience working a bakery setting, but she does have 'extensive racoon handling experience.'"

"You never know when that might come in handy," Zelda said sarcastically.

The other applicants were hardly any better, a mishmash of

magical folk that had all sorts of experience other than working in a bakery. "Maybe I'm being unfair. I didn't even bake before Constance handed the shop over to me."

"What's your intuition telling you?" Zelda asked me.

"It's telling me my princess is in another castle. Now that I think about it, this might be the worst time to try and hire someone. I don't have any money, I don't have a bakery, and half the town is convinced I'm poisoning people with my bakes."

"Judging by today's success I'd say it's more like 99% of the town," Zelda said without thinking. I gave her *the look* and she responded with a sheepish grin. "Sorry."

"Ugh, there's nothing to apologize for, you were only telling the truth." My phone pinged again then; another application having come through. "Hm, this one doesn't look all bad actually. *Mukondi Kasongo.*"

"They sound African," Zelda commented.

"She is," I said, looking over her resume. Mukondi had ten years of bakery experience, having ran her own bakery back in Nigeria. "She also says she is a master coffee brewer and bread baker."

"Why does she want to work for you?" Zelda laughed. "She should open her own place by the sounds of things!"

"I'm not sure, but I think I need to interview this one for sure." I starred the email and put my phone back into my pocket. "What should we do with the rest of the day?" I asked. "Fancy going to the movies? I'd love to sit in a dark room right now and blend into the shadows."

"I'm up for that," Zelda said. "Though I should probably head into the apartment first and put some food down for Rufio. I forgot to feed him this morning."

A few moments passed before I turned to look at Zelda. "Wait, who's Rufio?"

"My familiar," she said.

"You don't have a familiar!" I said.

"I do too. Though he's not really mine; he's kind of tied to the apartment. I guess I'm just temporarily looking after him while I live there."

"How have I not met this Rufio yet?" I asked.

"He's quite aloof. I leave his food up on the terrace. To be honest he's rarely ever in."

"Right... okay, well we can swing by the apartment and feed your nonexistent familiar first."

"He does exist!" she laughed.

Dropping by Zelda's apartment wasn't as simple as that though. When she opened the door, it didn't swing open in one easy motion. It Jluered, like a video that was buffering. "What the..." Zelda mumbled as we walked in.

"You have to help!" Hermes said, running into the living room as we entered. Again, like the door, his movement was all broken and janky, as if the universe itself was glitching out. Even his speech was stammered and weird sounding.

"What did you do?" I asked him.

"Not me! That owl of yours! She's messing everything up!" he said, his voice stammering again.

Zelda and I looked at one another and ran into the kitchen. Even though I was running I felt like I wasn't moving properly. As we came into the kitchen, we saw that everything was floating in the air. There on top of the fridge was Phoebe, the time owl, a bright white halo glowing around her.

"Uh, Phoebe, is everything okay?" I asked her.

"I'm sorry," she said, genuinely sounding remorseful. "I'm just a little tired is all. I've not slept properly since I arrived, and it's starting to effect the area around me."

"Oh gosh," I said, ducking as an egg-timer came floating towards my head. "This is all my fault, sorry. I should have sorted out your perch!"

"It's fine," Phoebe said, trying to sound upbeat. "I can hold things together a little longer."

"This is holding things together?" Zelda muttered to me.

"We'll go and get you a perch right now, or a cage. Which is better?" I asked the malfunctioning owl.

"If you can afford one, a cage, though it'll be pricey."

"I'll throw it on my credit card! We want you well rested, don't we?!" I laughed nervously. I looked at Hermes, my expression turning graver. "Can you hold the fort while we're gone?"

"Don't I always?" he said, his back paws lifting up in the air as he began to float too. "Just hurry up! She keeps summoning visions from my past, and I don't like it!"

I turned and looked at Zelda, gripping the doorframe as we both started to float too. "We need to get over to that pet shop in Wildwood, now. Can you help me?"

"Do I have a choice?!" she said as her head bumped against the ceiling.

* * *

Twenty minutes later we were on a ferry heading in the direction of Wildwood. The 'ferry' was actually just a small boat that could seat about ten. It was just me, Zelda, and the captain, Gordo, who had ferried me across the lake when I first arrived at Compass Cove.

Gordo was an old seadog with a penchant for shaggy dog stories. It was hard to separate fact from fiction when Gordo was concerned, and he liked to talk—at length.

"That's when I realized Victor Gumball was actually just a part of imagination, an alternate personality if you will," he said as he approached the end of a story that had begun when we hopped onto his boat at least twenty minutes ago. "When I was Victor, I went across the country setting up these fight clubs. In the end it all came crashing down when we demolished the American banking system via explosives."

Zelda and I glared at him for a moment. "That's just the plot to Fight Club," she said.

"Fight Club?" Gordo asked with the turn of his head.

"Yeah, Brad Pitt, Ed Norton," Zelda clarified.

"Never heard of it," Gordo said with a straight face. "Any good?"

Zelda just buried her head in her hands and sighed. "Why do I bother." She lifted her head and looked up at me. "How much longer until the police finish repairing the roads? I can't go on living like this!"

"I don't know, but it doesn't seem like it'll be done in a hurry."

Just before I arrived at Compass Cove a small earthquake caused landslides around the lake, knocking out the roads between the town on the north side of the lake and the other towns. Compass Cove town, which was on the north side, was currently separated from Wildwood and Eureka. The police didn't have the budget to hire professionals to clear the debris, so Burt and his boys were doing it themselves in their spare time—and it was taking *time*.

Not long after that we arrived at Wildwood. Zelda hopped off the boat, and I gave a begrudging thanks to Gordo for ferrying us. "Well, I better be off!" he said cheerily. "I've got a conference call with CNN News, and I can't be late!"

I rolled my eyes and smiled, unable to resist Gordo's peculiar charm. "Sure you do, Gordo. Good luck with that."

As I reached the end of the jetty and took my first steps onto land I looked up at the town of Wildwood. Before me was a dusty-looking little town, the kind that shoved most of its businesses onto one main street. I was actually surprised how different it was to Compass Cove town. "It feels like we've taken a step into rural America," I remarked. Wildwood looked just like a little sleepy town you'd find hidden in a pastoral southern state.

"Yeah, that's kind of the vibe out here," Zelda said as she pulled her hood up over her face. "Let's just git to the pet shop and we can hurry out of here."

"I'm sorry, did you just say *git*?" I laughed. "Are you a southern bumpkin? And why did you pull your hood over your face?"

"Quit your hollerin' and let's git this cage already!" Zelda said, hurrying toward Wildwood's main street. I hurried after her, my brow furrowing in confusion. She had her hands in her pockets, her head held low. There was no mistaking it, she was definitely trying to hide.

"Why are you talking like that?" I asked as I caught up to her.

"Like what?" she said, the distinctive southern drawl coming out more with each passing sentence.

"Like that! You sound like you're from Alabama, Zelda!"

"Hush up!" Zelda said, grabbing my arm and pulling me in close. "Don't say my name like that! Yer jabbering like a turkey on Thanksgiving!"

I just stared at my sister, utterly confounded by this accent change. "This is the best thing that has happened to me since moving here."

"Look, the accent just sort of takes over whenever I come back here, alright? I can't help it!"

"But what's with the hood? Why are you sneaking around?!"

"Because I don't want anyone to spot me, obviously! Everyone around here knows who I am, and if Nana Bucktooth finds out I'm here, we won't be getting out of here anytime soon!"

"I have no idea what you're talking about, but I am immensely fascinated," I said.

Zelda sighed and pulled me into a side alley between two shops. One was *Big Bob's Boot Emporium* and the other was *Del's Dollar Store*.

"Nana Bucktooth runs things around here, and she's also my Maw Maw."

"I'm sorry, Maw Maw?" I said, barely able to contain my laughter. "Did I wander onto the set of Little House on the Prairie?"

"Look I already told you there are two main witching families around Compass Cove lake, there's the Wicks, and the Brewers. Neither side likes the other, but I just happened to be stuck smack bang between the two."

"Wait, I remember you telling me this," I recalled. Zelda and I were only half-sisters. My mother had me first with a mortal man out west when she was traveling on the road. She never told anyone back here about me, and she ended up in a mental hospital shortly after giving birth to me.

After that she came home to Compass Cove and had another baby girl with Billy Brewer. Mom disappeared again, and to this day no one knows where she went. That second baby girl was Zelda, who spent her time being raised by the Brewers and the Wicks, so she had two grandmothers—my grandmother Liza, and this mysterious Nana Bucktooth, whom I had yet to meet.

We still had no idea what had happened to our mother; she was an enigmatic character, and even Grandmother Liza—my mom's mother—didn't have the full picture on her daughter.

"Then you'll know the best thing is for us to get the cage and get out of here. Nana Bucktooth always wants something, and she'll be pitching a fit because I ain't been to visit enough!" Zelda said.

By this point Zelda's southern twang was no longer a twang, but a full-blown drawl. "I'm beginning to struggle to understand what you're saying, but okay. Let's get to this pet shop and hurry back."

As Zelda was technically helping me out here I decided to try and pay respects to the fact that she didn't want to get spotted while here in Wildwood. I must admit I was curious to meet the Brewer family. They seemed to have an infamous reputation, and I wanted to see what the other half of Zelda's family was like, but I had to keep in mind there was a time owl back at my apartment, and the fabric of reality itself was starting to come undone—time was literally of the essence.

A few minutes later we arrived at the pet shop. I was about to head through the entrance when Zelda yanked me back, pulling me in the direction of the alleyway.

"Hey, what gives!" I shouted.

"That's the human entrance," she grumbled from under her hood. "The witch entrance is around here." Zelda pulled me down another side alley, stopping in front of a rusted metal service door that looked like it hadn't been opened in years. She took her wand out, tapped it against the metal and the metal transformed into a beautiful wooden door with painted glass paneling. Zelda twisted its ornate brass handle and we headed inside.

"It's bigger on the inside!" I remarked.

As we stepped in, I saw a room that was much taller than the one-story building we'd approached from the street. Everywhere I looked I saw cages and tanks of all sizes, containing all sorts of magical looking creatures. A cacophony of sound filled the air, and bright dashes of color moved within every little enclosure. The smell of sawdust lingered in the air.

"Feels like backstage at a circus, huh?" Zelda said as she walked through the sprawling aisles. I felt as if I could spend hours in here and not see everything.

"Welcome to Zambo's Pet Shop!" a large mustachioed man announced as he sprung from nowhere. He was wearing a white shirt, tweed trousers, boots, and suspenders. His head was bald and shiny. "I am Zambo. I've not seen you around here before. New in town?"

"Zora," I began, but Zelda dug her elbow into my ribs. "Ow! I mean, Zena, Zena Wax."

"Welcome, Zena Wax!" Zambo said, putting air quotes around the name. Our attempt at being covert wasn't so subtle it appeared. "And what can I help you with today? You have the look of someone with urgency about you."

"I need a cage for an Olaphax, that's a time—"

"Time owl," Zambo said, "Yes, I'm familiar. Very rare creatures, beautiful birds, though they can be trouble if they do not get enough sleep."

"That's exactly my issue!"

"Oh my," Zambo said with a concerned turn of his head. "How bad is it?"

"Time is jittering and things are floating in the kitchen, but it's all confined to my sister's apartment so far."

Zambo's eyes suddenly shot to Zelda's cloaked figure. So far Zelda hadn't said anything; she was just staring intently at the tiles on the floor. "I see. Well that sounds pretty bad already. As it happens, I have a few items that might do the job. Follow me."

We followed Zambo into the shop, heading deeper into the seemingly endless room of packed shelves. I wondered how something this large could exist within a building so small from the outside. Looking around I couldn't see any walls at the edge of the room now.

A few minutes later Zambo stopped in a dark and dusty aisle, which was long and bordered by two tall shelves that stretched up to the ceiling above us. "Here," he said, coming to a stop with a pivot. He gestured to the space ahead, in which there was a silver cage and a perch.

"It's perfect!" I said. "How much?"

"For you, Zora Wick, I can cut you a nice deal."

My eyes widened as he said my real name. "You know me?"

"I like the newspaper. Guilty as charged. I don't believe you did it however. I wouldn't take your custom otherwise. I had heard there was a new Wick witch in town."

"You don't know anything about me," I said. "How can you be so sure of my innocence?"

"The Wicks are a long and noble line, not a shred of darkness about them. Those Brewers however…" Zambo reached forward and snatched back Zelda's hood, revealing her face.

"Hey!" she protested, her drawl stronger than ever.

Zambo just crossed his arms and shook his head, laughing to himself. "Zelda Brewer, I knew it was you the moment you came in here. Long time since I've seen you in Wildwood. Does Nana Bucktooth know you're here?"

"No, she doesn't. And that's just about the way it's going to stay, y'all here? Now help my sister out. We need to get this cage and skedaddle out of here," Zelda said. I couldn't help but stare at her in fascination. She sounded like an extra from an old cowboy movie.

Zambo looked back at me. "The cage is yours for free, on the condition you help me out with something at a later date."

"Me?" I asked. "What makes you think I'd be able to help you out with anything?"

The large bald-headed man coughed, and a small monkey suddenly appeared on his shoulder, looking like it had materialized from the thin air itself. Half of the monkey was black, the other half was white, a jagged line splitting the color down the middle from its head to tail. On the black side the monkey had a white eye, and on the white side its eye was black.

"What the heck is that thing?" I asked.

"Oh crap, it's Juju," Zelda groaned. "I didn't realize you still had him."

"I do," Zambo said with a boastful grin. "Zora this is Juju, a Harlequin Marmoset. Beautiful little creatures, gifted with the ability of telepathy. He tells me everything. Like how Zelda didn't want anyone to recognize her, and her wanting to keep it a secret that you're a Prismatic Witch."

"Oh... fiddlesticks," I murmured.

Zambo just laughed. "Fear not, your secret is safe with me. Like I said, the cage is yours for free. I only ask that you help me out with something when I ask. It's a small problem, but I'm afraid there's nothing that can be done about it right this moment."

"Okay," I said. "It's a deal. Please, keep the Prismatic thing to yourself."

Zambo mimed zipping his lips shut. "Now, was there anything else you needed today?"

As it was just the cage, we followed Zambo to the register, where he boxed up the cage and handed it to me. We said goodbye and made our way outside to catch the ferry back to Compass Cove town.

"That could have been much worse," Zelda hissed as she threw her hood back up. "Now let's git to that dock and hurry out of here. I don't want—"

As we came around the corner onto the street, Zelda walked head-first into a man wearing not much else apart from dungarees and a broad-brimmed straw hat. Zelda flew back and hit the ground, her hood coming down as she did.

The man instantly began berating Zelda in a thick southern twang. "Watch where 'yer goin, you darn city slick—" He paused, took his hat off, and slapped it against his leg. "Well I'll be a barrel full of rattlesnakes. Zelda, git on over here!"

In another move he yanked Zelda up into a hug, one that seemed to crush all the air from her lungs. "Yeehaw!" he said. "I didn't know you were back! Let's have a party, I'll fire up the grill and call the others!"

Zelda squirmed out of the man's grasp, trying to straighten her hair out as she did so. "Actually, I ain't sticking around—" she began, but the man cut in to grab my hand and shake it.

"Sweet John's the name!" he said. "Sweet John Brewer!"

"Zora," I replied. "Zora Wick."

Sweet John's lips rounded, and a look of surprise came over him, like he was meeting a celebrity. "The killer! From the paper! What a treat!"

"Alleged killer," I mumbled. "Zel, who is this?"

"Zora this is Sweet John Brewer, one of my dad's sons."

Sweet John started laughing like a donkey—I finally understood where Zelda got it from—slapping his leg and wiping his eyes as if it was the funniest thing he'd ever heard. "One of his sons! Can you believe that!" he said, taking Zelda in under his arm and rubbing his knuckles over her head. "Old Zel here always had a way of looking at things funny. A much simpler way of sayin' things is that she's my sister!"

CHAPTER 13

"Now just a darn' tootin' moment," I said to Sweet John Brewer and Zelda. I didn't have the same southern drawl as either of them, but I wanted to be part of the fun. "Zelda, you never told me you had other siblings? I thought I was the first!"

"Oh, ol' Zelly here is just embarrassed by us is all!" Sweet John said, Zelda still underneath his arm as he ruffled her hair with his free hand. "We Brewers is everywhere, ain't that right, Zelly!"

'Zelly' managed to squeeze herself from the arm of her brother, Sweet John Brewer, yanking her hood back over her face again as she glared at him. "Can you stop messing up my hair? Y'all know I hate that!"

"Ah shucks, sis. I'm just excited to see you is all! What's it been? Almost a year now! Nana Bucktooth is fixing to see you something crazy!" Sweet John hollered.

"Well she can keep fixing!" Zelda said, almost spitting the words. "Every time I come around here, I just end up getting in a whole big bucket of trouble!"

"I am deeply fascinated by everything that is happening right now," I said, a huge grin plastered on my face. Zelda shot me a derisive look and continued.

"Look, John, it's good to see you, but we've gotta get going. We've got problems with a time owl. Come over to Compass Cove town sometime, ya hear?" Without even waiting for a response Zelda spun on her heels and started marching down the sidewalk. Sweet John didn't miss a beat. He jumped forward and grabbed Zelda, wrapping her in another affectionate headlock.

"Now, now! Where do you think yer going so fast, missy?! You can't just swing through town without stopping by to say hi to everyone else!" Sweet John said. Zelda spun out of his grasp, looking thoroughly incensed.

"I can and I will! I already told you we've got places to be. As for the matter of you seeing me here, Nana Bucktooth doesn't have to hear about that!" Zelda hooted.

"Hear about what?" a graveled voice came from behind us. Turning around I saw a short, stout woman, with a patch over her right eye. She was wearing an old paisley dress, huge black combat boots, and sitting along her back there was a rifle that was nearly the size she was.

I don't know why, but I felt intrinsic fear.

"Nana Bucktooth!" Zelda stammered. "What are you doing off the ranch?!"

The old woman spat into a sewer grate, narrowed her good eye, and hustled over to us. "Doing more walking. Doctor says I need to do more of that. Sweet John here got me one of those watches from China," she said, gesturing to a smart watch on her wrist. "Says I gotta do all this walking. Well I don't like it. Those Chinese don't tell me what to do!"

"I already told you, Maw Maw, it's an activity tracker!" Sweet John said. "Ain't got nothing to do with the Chinese!" Without look- ing, Nana Bucktooth swiped her hand out and struck Sweet John on the side of the head. He yelped and shrank back. "Sorry, Maw Maw!"

"Where have you been?" she said, aiming the question at Zelda.

"Busy in Compass Cove. Running the café with Celeste."

"You got business to run here," Nana Bucktooth said. "Yer' wasting your life running around with those Wicks. They'll do you no good. Family business needs you."

"Nana, I got my own life now!" Zelda protested. "And Dilby said if I get in trouble in this town again—"

"Don't you worry about Sheriff Dilby!" Nana Bucktooth snapped. "You think he runs this town? I run this town!" Sweet John cautiously advanced on Nana Bucktooth, lingering at her side. She turned and scowled at him. "Why you hovering, boy?!"

"Nana, it's almost time for your show. We're going to miss it!" Sweet John said submissively.

The old woman shook her head. "Listen fast, Zelly, because I don't want to miss my show. We're gonna git, but you're gonna come and visit, you hear? If you don't come to me, I'll come to you."

"You're not allowed in Compass Cove town!" Zelda said. "You made a treaty!"

Nana Bucktooth just cackled. "You think I care 'bout a treaty? That town wouldn't even be there if it wasn't for the work me and the family does. You come and visit. I wanna see that little face in the next week, or I'm coming to you. That clear?"

"Yes, Nana," Zelda mumbled.

"There a mouse in your mouth, girl?!"

"Yes, Nana!" Zelda said more clearly. Nana Bucktooth turned and, for the first time, took notice of me.

"As for you," she said in a low growl.

"What did I do?!" I said defensively.

"I know who you are, another Wick. I seen your face all over them papers. So you're a killer, eh?"

"Alleged killer," I said.

The curmudgeonly old woman actually smirked. "Yer Prismatic too," she said, scowling.

I gulped. "Uh, how did you know that?"

"You think I got to this age by being stupid, girl? Is that what you think I am, stupid?"

"No, I didn't—!"

Nana Bucktooth threw her head back and started laughing. "I'm yanking yer chain, *Wick*. You might be one of them, but you didn't grow up under that rat Liza, so maybe you ain't so bad. I want you to come too when Zelly swings by, you hear? I need help with something, and I figure yer just the one for the job. So you can come? Brilliant!"

I hadn't even responded. Nana Bucktooth took the liberty of doing that for me. She didn't really seem to care what I was going to say either. She turned away from me and looked at Sweet John. "Oh Sweet John, where's the truck?" she asked in a sweet singsong voice that was out of odds with her regular barbed cadence.

"It's down the block, Maw," Sweet John answered diligently.

"Then go and get it before I miss my shows!" she growled, swinging for him again with the back of her hand. This time Sweet John ducked out of the way and started sprinting down the sidewalk, hollering his apologies as he did so. Within a minute he came back, an old rusted pickup truck screeching to a halt on the street. Nana Bucktooth got in without saying another word to either of us, and then they took off racing, their truck spitting up dust as they left.

"She was… a treat," I said, spluttering on the dust left in the air.

"Just wait until you see her in a bad mood," Zelda said out of the side of her mouth. "She was surprisingly chipper today. That walking must be doing her some good."

"That was her being chipper?" I asked with alarm.

Zelda just nodded her head slowly, looking as though she was still winding down from the interaction. "Yeah, trust me. You just met Nana Bucktooth on a good day." Zelda squinted at something down the block and threw her hood over her face again. "Darn it, I think Big Tabby's coming this way. She's one of my aunts. We better get out of here before someone else corners us, otherwise we'll never leave!" Zelda grabbed my hand and we started running for the dock. I kind of wanted to stay and meet the rest of her hillbilly family, but Zelda was right.

A magical owl was currently dismantling Zelda's apartment, and if we didn't hurry home, we'd have much bigger problems to worry about!

* * *

Upon getting back to the apartment we found things were *much* worse, but as soon as Phoebe was in her cage the issues abated immediately. Hermes, who had been floating in the living room, came crashing to the ground with a yelp. Phoebe fell asleep in her cage straight away, and everything else went back to normal.

Zelda's southern twang disappeared somewhere on the ferry ride back to Compass Cove, but the genie was out of the bottle now; I could never unhear it. After making a quick bite to eat we sat down in the living room and put the television on. Hermes strolled in after a while and jumped up into my lap.

"You have more applicants, by the way," Hermes said to me.

"What are you talking about?" I asked him.

"For the ad you left in the paper. You got more emails!"

"How do you know anything about that?"

"I was using your laptop while you were both running around in Wildwood playing Witches of Hazard."

"You know the password to my laptop?"

"Of course I do. I spied it the other day when you were logging on! I don't know if you know this, Zora, but you mumble under your breath when you're typing. That's a serious security flaw."

"It's true, you do," Zelda said.

"Okay, let's put aside the idea of me being angry with you for hacking into my laptop and snooping through my things. What are the applicants like?"

Hermes made a huge raspberry sound. "They stink! But there was one that looked half-decent."

"What was their name?"

"Daphne Romero," Hermes said proudly. "And get this, she used to be the baking assistant at Marjorie Slade's place, you know, before it got shut down because Marjorie Slade tried to kill you and Zelda."

"Yes, I vaguely recall, what with it only being a month ago."

"Daphne's a really good baker, Zora," Zelda said to me. "She's a really kind witch too, always helping out with the local community."

"I do feel kind of bad putting her out of a job," I muttered. It hadn't even occurred to me until just now that having Marjorie arrested would have closed Daphne's place of work.

"Don't feel bad. You never even met the broad!" Hermes countered.

"I did meet her. We talked briefly when I went into the shop to visit Marjorie—before I knew she was a killer of course. I actually got on with Daphne really well and—" I paused mid-sentence, a flashback coming to me suddenly as I recalled something.

"Well, what?" Hermes said, rolling his eyes. "Come on, don't leave us hanging!"

"It's weird. I remember having this vision when I was in the bakery, before I re-opened officially. I was in the front of the bakery, it was bustling, and I called into the back to ask someone for help. The name I called was Daphne."

"That about settles it then," Zelda said. "Daphne has to be the one!"

"Hang on a moment now. I've not even interviewed yet; we can't be sure. There was that other applicant, remember, the one from Africa? She had a great resume too."

"I saw that one," Hermes said. "She looked pretty great as well. Still, *technically* you don't even have a bakery at the moment, and with your face all over the papers you won't be selling cakes to pay wages any time soon." I glared at Hermes. "What?!"

"I suppose you're only being truthful. Still, *Bitz and Bosch* will be done at the bakery tomorrow, so things are starting to look up from here. I will have to dedicate some time to clearing my name though."

"I can't believe it. He was telling the truth!" Zelda said, grabbing for the remote and turning the volume up on the TV.

"What is it?" Hermes said, spinning around on my lap to face the screen. "Don't tell me, they're bringing back Golden Girls!"

I looked up at the screen; the program we had been watching was now done, and the news had come on. There on the screen was Gordo, the sailor with a penchant for shaggy dog stories. The last thing he'd said when I saw him today is that he had an interview with the news. I thought he'd just been lying.

"Man, is that the crazy old guy from the lake? I don't know where the truth starts and the lies end with that guy," Hermes said. "I once overheard him telling this tourist couple that he used to own a shrimp trawler with Marlon Brando."

"Quiet!" Zelda said. "They're talking!"

The three of us focused on the interview as Zelda turned the volume up.

"And here we are with Gordo Pascall," the news reporter said. "Gordo, you've been a fisherman around these parts almost all your life. I bet you must have some interesting stories. What can you tell us about Compass Cove and it's rich history?"

A twinkle formed in Gordo's eye, and I let out a breath. "Oh boy, here we go," I said.

"Miriam, I'm glad you asked," Gordo said. The reporter had very clearly introduced herself as *Gillian.* "I've actually got a great story about the time we ousted the abominable squid from Compass Cove lake, but before I get into that story, I have an announcement to make!"

"Of course," the news reporter said. "And what would you like to say?"

"I got married this week, there's my wife over there, god bless her soul. Honey, get over here!" Gordo pointed excitedly to someone off-camera. Gillian, the reporter, filled the air as Gordo's mysterious wife made her way into the frame and stepped in beside him. As she appeared on the screen Zelda, Hermes, and I all started screaming in shock.

"It's Celeste!" Zelda said. She had jumped up to her feet and was pointing at the TV in horror. "Celeste married Gordo? What?! He's like one hundred years older than her! Zora, what's happening? What's happening?!"

"I don't know. I can't hear because you won't stop screaming!" I grabbed the remote from Zelda and turned the TV up some more.

"—that's right, just two days ago, Gillian!" Celeste laughed nervously. "I guess I was just drawn to his soul. It was love at first sight!"

116

"That explains her suspicious activity," I muttered.

"I knew there was no foot doctor!" Zelda roared, still standing on the couch for some reason.

Hermes was just laughing to himself. "What's so funny?" I asked him.

"Man, I am so grateful for living amongst you idiots. There's never a dull moment!"

I didn't agree with Hermes often, but there was no denying it— something odd was always going on in Compass Cove.

CHAPTER 14

*D*espite our best efforts no one was able to get hold of Celeste. She wasn't answering her phone, and even her sister, Sabrina, was having no luck. Needless to say, we spent the better part of the evening talking back and forth about the shocking revelation—I mean, why would a young healthy girl like Celeste want to marry an old pathological liar like Gordo? There had to be something at play here.

The following morning, I woke up bright and early to go and check on the bakery. Zelda was scheduled to be in the café with Celeste that morning and she got out the door even before I did, keen to find out why our cousin had married a geriatric fisherman.

I arrived at my bakery a few minutes after nine, a chipper pep in my step as I walked down the alleyway to the rear entrance. As I came around the back I saw the huge figure of Bosch.

"Morning!" I said cheerily. "How did the clear out go?"

"Two more day," Bosch said without returning a smile. He dropped some heavy looking boxes onto the ground and disappeared through the back door without saying so much as another word.

"Um, hello?!" I shouted. I wondered if it was safe to go inside, but the big guy had just done so without hesitancy, so why not? I marched through the back door and saw sheets of plastic hanging from every surface. The interior of the building was lit with curious lavender light that made it look like the air itself was sparkling. From upstairs I heard Italian opera music. I followed the stairs up to my apartment, where I found Bitz with a blowtorch in one hand and some sort of magical cage contraption in the other.

"Hi!" I said loudly, trying to make myself heard over the opera music. "It's been three days!"

"Ah, Miss Wick, hello!" Bitz said, looking up at me briefly before he brought his blowtorch back to a Crème Brule on the countertop. "Bosch just said he saw you outside!"

"Yeah, I came back to reclaim my bakery. You said three days!"

"Yes, I'm afraid we may have been a little optimistic with our timeline!" Bitz suddenly transformed into the mammoth Bosch, who set down the blowtorch and cage. He thundered across the apartment, picked up what looked like an old deep-sea diver helmet and carried it back to the kitchen, setting it down on the table with a thud. He shifted back into Bitz, who returned to the cage and the Crème Brule.

"What's that supposed to mean?" I asked, watching as he placed the little glass jar inside the helmet. He put the cage on top. Looking around the room I realized there were little jars of Crème Brule everywhere. The glittering lavender fog made it hard to think straight. Coupled with the loud opera music I felt as though I was in some fever dream.

"You asked for nonlethal extraction, and sometimes that takes longer. Don't worry though; we're making great progress!"

"And all of this?" I said, gesturing to the puzzling and seemingly random nature of their work.

"Poxy hate opera music, but they *love* Crème Brule. We lure them out with this. The opera music and the magical fog reduces their inhibitions."

"So you're effectively getting them drunk and baiting them with munchies?" I said.

"It's a delicate scientific process," Bitz said with a sage nod. "Yes, I'm afraid we'll need two more days. Did you need anything?"

"No… I guess I'll just… go then?"

Bitz again transformed back into Bosch, who thundered back into the apartment without acknowledgement. I turned and left, wondering if I'd ever forget the absolute insanity that I'd just witnessed. As I got back to my van my phone started ringing. I didn't recognize the number, but I figured it might be an applicant for the assistant position, so I took the call.

"Hello?" I asked.

"Under your windshield wipers," the voice said. "That's the front page for tomorrow."

I noticed then that something *was* tucked under the wipers. I pulled out the paper and unfolded it. Sure enough there was a mock front page for the *Compass Cove Bugle*. There was a headline that read, 'DID ALLEGED POISONER HAVE AFFAIR WITH DECEASED?' Along with a photograph of me that looked like it had been taken on the street at some point yesterday. I looked unreasonably angry in the photo.

"Who is this?" I growled down the phone.

"Let's just say I'm someone that can make life very unpleasant for you," the caller responded. They were definitely a woman and judging by the nasal New Jersey accent I had my suspicions who the anonymous caller was.

"This is Carla King, isn't it?" I asked.

The caller sputtered. "How did you know?!"

"You sound exactly like your brother. Now what is this? Are you blackmailing me? I barely knew Mark Mobson. I had nothing to do with him!"

"Doesn't look like that from where I'm sitting," Carla said. "I want info, or this headline goes out tomorrow."

"This is slander!" I shouted down the phone. "I wasn't having an affair with the guy; you can't just print lies!"

"Oh, I'm not, but that pretty little word keeps me off the hook. I didn't say you had an affair; I said *allegedly*."

"Who's your source?" I growled.

"Honey, this is the *Compass Cove Bugle*, not the *New York Times*, I don't need a source. All I have to say is an anonymous birdie gave this to me!"

"So you're literally just making up lies and printing them."

"Unless you give me some truth."

"What do you want?"

"An interview, with you. Thirty minutes, no limits!" Carla demanded.

I scoffed. "So you can twist my words into headlines for another week? Not a chance. I might be naïve, but I'm not stupid. I know how you reporters work."

"Then I guess I'll just have to go with this story for tomorrow's cover. How's business been since you became Compass Cove's most infamous baker?"

"Just fine," I said through gritted teeth. It had, of course, been horrible, but I didn't want to admit as much to a bottom-feeder like Carla King.

"Two grand, thirty minutes of your time. Clear your name. A chance to redeem your reputation!" Carla offered.

"We're done here. Contact me again and you'll be hearing from my lawy—" I paused, realizing my lawyer was Carla's brother, someone *she* was spying on. "Uh, on second thought scratch that. I'll get a new lawyer, and you'll hear from *them*."

"Don't you kick Kenny to the curb! He's a good boy! Give him a chance!" Carla protested.

"Stop spying on him then and stop blackmailing me!" I hung up the phone without another word, wishing it was a conventional handset so I could slam it into a receiver. I stared at my reflection in the van's window, realizing that I *did* look unfathomably angry. "Man, I really have to work on my resting b-face."

A few seconds of calm passed before the phone started ringing again. I didn't even look at the screen this time. I just answered, jumping straight to fury.

"Listen here, you shrew! I don't care what you put in the paper; if you're going to make this personal then I can play at that game too! You're not the only one with claws! Is that clear?!" I snapped.

For a second there was no response then a gentle-voiced man spoke. "Um… is this Zora Wick?"

Sheer horror spread throughout me as I realized what I had done. It wasn't Carla calling me back to threaten me some more; it was a complete stranger.

"This is she!" I laughed nervously, instantly adopting a brighter and cheerier tone. "Sorry about that, I thought you were… someone else!"

"I see that," the man said. He cleared his throat and continued. "Ahem, my name is Amos, Amos Aposhine, I'm calling from *Compass Cove Community School of Magic*. Is this a bad time?"

I froze. "No, no! This is a perfect time. There couldn't be a more perfect time!"

"Right," Amos said down the line. "Anyway, I'm calling to say that we received your application. Congratulations, you passed with flying colors. We'd be happy to welcome you into our facility."

"You would? I did? Oh my gosh, I—I don't know what to say!"

"You don't have to say anything," Amos said, sounding much warmer now. "We'll send an orientation package via owl. It should be with you in the next day or so. The new term starts in four weeks, so if all goes well, we'll be seeing you very soon."

"I—thank you," I blurted, a little overwhelmed with shock. "Thank you, thank you!"

"Alright," Amos said, chuckling. "I'll have to go now, more people to call. See you soon, Zora Wick!"

For a few moments I was riding a high. The last few days had been one bad moment to another. This was the first bit of good news I'd received in a tide of unfortunate luck. Turning around to get into the van I let out a scream as I saw Blake standing behind me.

"For the love of lemons!" I yelped, throwing my arms up helplessly and dropping my phone. Blake's hand swiped through the air quickly and caught it before it hit the ground.

"Sorry," he said, "didn't mean to scare you."

"So—you were just standing silently behind me for the fun of it?" I said sarcastically.

"I move very quietly; I forget that sometimes."

"Do it again and I'm getting you a collar with a bell. What did you want anyway?"

"I checked out that little problem of yours," he said, then adding for clarity, "the mob thing?"

"Yes, it kind of goes without saying. What did you dig up?"

"I think I found our real suspect. Let's go and get a drink somewhere and we can talk it over."

* * *

BLAKE HOPPED IN THE VAN, and we drove to a quiet little coffee shop at the edge of town. We grabbed a table upstairs, a window providing a nice view of the street below and the lake beyond.

"Okay, start yammering," I said as I took a sip of my hot chocolate. Blake pulled his chair around so he was sitting next to me and produced a thin yellow folder.

"Have you ever heard of Donnie The Face?" Blake said as he opened up the folder, revealing a myriad of photographs all taken in black and white. In each one of them there was a man of Italian American descent. He was either in a tracksuit, or a dress suit.

"Did you take these pictures?" I asked.

"Yeah, I've been tailing this guy since we last spoke."

I blinked. "What happened to taking pictures with a smartphone?"

Blake looked at me like I was crazy. "Can we focus on the bigger picture here? If you must know, I don't really like technology all that much. Traditional film camera suits me fine."

"Okay, grandpa," I laughed. "So, who is Donnie The Face?"

"Small-time local mobster, had connections with Mark Mobson."

"Involved in the club?"

"*Was*. Donnie withdrew his investment about a year ago."

"How do you know all this?" I asked.

"Let's just say people start talking when you dangle them headfirst over the edge of a highway."

"You dangled this guy over a highway?" I asked, wondering if I should fear Blake a little.

"Not this guy, one of his grunts," Blake said calmly.

I gulped. "I didn't realize you were that type of cop," I croaked.

"Zora, I don't know if you realize, but your life is under threat here. It's my job to protect you, at all costs. Besides, these aren't run of the mill folk—they're criminals."

"Okay, just… maybe be a little more legal with your investigating going forward?" I asked, phrasing the question as gently as I could.

Blake looked at me for a moment then nodded. "Okay, I can do that for you."

"So, this Donnie guy withdrew his investment from Mark's club a year ago. Do we know why?"

"Yeah, because Mark slept with Donnie The Face's wife."

"Ah, that'll do it," I said. "Still, it was a year ago, right? Why would Donnie wait that long to retaliate by poisoning Mark?"

"Because an old wound was just re-opened. The divorce between Donnie and his wife finalized a few days ago; the day before Mark Mobson died to be precise."

"So mob guy invests in club. Club owner sleeps with his wife, mob guy divorces wife, then he poisons guy that slept with his wife."

"That's the gist of it," Blake nodded.

"I have to admit the timing is suspicious," I said.

"You haven't even heard the best part. Donnie The Face owns a factory that processes chemicals for pharmaceutical purposes. I dug around there a little and the factory stores strychnine."

I let out a long whistle. "Wow, Blake, we might have a bullseye here. I should show this stuff to the police, right?"

"I mean, I *am* the police. I've gotten as close to this as I can, Zora. There's nothing concrete here to put Donnie away, but it's a starting point. If we can find the smoking gun, we could lock this guy up."

"What does the smoking gun look like here?" I asked.

Blake shrugged. "I don't know, but we'll know when we see it."

"Or not," a voice said. Looking up we both saw Hudson standing over our table. Blake immediately jumped to his feet, his fists clenched at his side.

"You?!" Blake hissed. "You're working with them, aren't you?"

Hudson just laughed and pulled up a seat, sitting down at the table with us. I jerked Blake back into his seat by tugging on his sleeve.

"I'm going to preface this interaction with a warning," I said. "Either of you so much as looks at the other funny and I'm out of here. Clear?"

"I don't trust you one bit," Blake said to Hudson. "No human can sneak up on a werewolf. Just what the hell are you?"

"I'm afraid that's classified," Blake said. He turned and looked at me. "Zora, it's good to see you."

"What are you doing here, Hudson?" I asked. He pulled out a phone and slid it across the table to me. I took it and the screen lit up, showing photos of a large Black man in a boxing gym. "What is this?"

"Research. I've been looking into Mobson for you, just like I said I would. That's a burner phone; you can keep it. Photos, videos, maps plotting Tyson Lemar's daily movements. I bugged him, so I know where he is at all times."

"And who this guy exactly?" I asked.

"This is the guy that killed Mark Mobson," Hudson said.

CHAPTER 15

"*R*idiculous," Blake scoffed. "I already found the guy that killed Mark Mobson. It's Donnie The Face. Mobson had an affair with his wife, Donnie and his wife divorced *this week*, and Donnie has access to strychnine."

Hudson faked a yawn. "Oh, sorry? Were you talking?"

Blake balled his fists and clenched his jaw. "If words aren't getting into that thick skull of yours, I can think of other ways of communicating."

"Trust the werewolf to jump straight to violence," Hudson said with a roll of his eyes.

"That's enough. Both of you quit," I said. "One more outburst and I'm out of here. Blake, let Hudson talk. You told me about your findings; now let him do the same."

"Just saying, I already looked into this. It's pointless," Blake murmured.

"Well, I looked into it *better*, dog boy." Hudson looked back at me and his phone of information.

"So why do you think this Tyson Lemar is our culprit? Is he another business partner of Mobson?"

"Sort of. Tyson Lemar is a local boxer. Used to fight in Vegas, he was big-time for a while. He's older now and retired, but he still runs a boxing gym down on the lake."

"Great gym," Blake said. "And Lemar's a great boxer. Great left hook."

"You know this guy?" I asked Blake.

"Not really," Blake said with a shrug. "A few of my cousins trained at the gym. I went once or twice. Lemar's a good guy though, definitely not a killer."

"Well, even good guys can go bad," Hudson explained, swiping to another photo on his phone. It was a screenshot of an online news article from a few months ago. *'Daughter of boxing legend found dead after overdose.'*

"What happened?" I asked Hudson.

"So, Tyson Lemar had this daughter, her name was Phoenix. Anyway, Phoenix was something of a socialite in Compass Cove. Big event? New club opening? She was there, the life and soul of the party. She was a regular at Mobson's club, *Angel*, and she struck up a friendship with Mobson. Apparently, she made it onto Mobson's payroll as a regular VIP."

"He paid her to come to the club?" I asked. "Why?"

"Because she got other people in the door. She was basically advertising the joint for him. Anyway, apparently Mobson has a pretty nasty possessive streak in him. He started to put up walls around Phoenix; he wanted her all to himself. He used his club to move heavy drugs, and he used those drugs to have power over people. He'd get them hooked and put them into his debt."

"Sounds like a real charmer," I murmured.

"He had a track record of doing this. He'd get young girls into the club, get them hooked on drugs, and then have them work in one of his strip clubs to make them pay back the money. He'd keep these girls as girlfriends as well, real piece of work. Several girls ended up overdosing in Mobson's clubs, and Phoenix was one of them."

"I'm guessing once this all came out Tyson Lemar wasn't too happy…" I said.

"You're right. Lemar tried to kill Mobson once already. He

attacked him in the street, nearly beat the guy to death. Fortunately for Mobson, his goons managed to step in just in time. Tyson Lemar was under house arrest for the last three months; that sentence expired just two weeks ago."

"So now Tyson is out and free, looking for revenge."

"Yup, and get this. His brother owns an animal control company. Lemar would have ready access to poisons like strychnine."

I took a few moments to consider the torrent of information that both Blake and Hudson had brought to me this morning.

"I still think it's Donnie The Face," Blake said, breaking the silence.

"Or it could be my guy, Tyson Lemar," Hudson replied, glaring at Blake. I could tell the two of them were just raring to go again, looking to swing their fists around for any old reason to prove who the bigger 'alpha' was.

"I'm getting tired of hearing you both squabble," I said, shutting down their arguing yet again. "Look, I think *both* of these guys could be potential suspects."

"Potential?" Hudson and Blake said at the same time.

"You're dismissing this?" Hudson asked. Blake looked at me, the same question in his eyes.

"I'm not dismissing anything, but from where I'm sitting it looks like this is only the tip of the iceberg. Mobson had a lot of enemies, right? There's a whole host of people that might have had reason to kill him. I think I want to look into this myself."

"Zora, you can't do that. If the mob catches you sneaking around —" Hudson began.

"Then what? Everyone else might be scared of them, but I'm not. They're a couple of men with guns. I've got a friggen' magic wand."

"I don't know where this energy is coming from, but I'm digging it," Hudson said with a smile.

"Someone's been following you," Blake said to me.

"Yeah? A werewolf cop?" I said.

"No, someone else."

"From the mob?"

He shook his head. "I don't think so. Some wiry little woman. I think she works at the paper."

"Carla King," I said. "She's the one that leaked the story in the first place. Her brother is my attorney, and she tapped his phone."

"You believe him?" Hudson asked.

"This attorney is a sleazeball, but he did genuinely seem surprised that the story leaked." I looked at Blake. "If that woman sees me poking around Mobson's clubs she'll put those photographs right in the paper."

"Exactly. It won't look good."

I drummed my fingers on the table. Damnit, how was I supposed to look into this case without anyone seeing me?

"I could scare her out of town for a few days?" Blake suggested. "Maybe set fire to her car?" I gave Blake a long look. "Or... not?"

"Remember that conversation we had about staying in the realms of the law? Remember the badge you're wearing."

Blake looked down at his officer's uniform. "I'm not really a cop, you know. This is just a cover so I can stay closer to you."

"Oh yeah, let's assign the chaotic werewolf as a protector, real smart," Hudson said sarcastically.

"And what do you propose we do?" Blake growled.

"It's simple. We create a diversion. If this reporter is looking somewhere else, it frees up Zora to investigate properly," Hudson said.

"Not the worst idea either of you knuckleheads have had..." I said. "What were you thinking?"

"I could blow something up downtown," Blake offered. "A car, or a van. Something small."

I stared at him again. "Let's make this easy. None of my plans will ever involve blowing things up or setting them on fire."

Blake soured. "Fine, whatever."

"What do you think?" I said to Hudson.

"How long do you need?" he asked.

"Maybe an hour or two."

"An hour or two to look around the club?" Hudson asked with surprise.

"I'm not sneaking around the club. I've got something else in mind." I pulled out one of the papers from the file that Blake had prepared for me. "It says here that Mark Mobson was married for fifteen years to one Sally DeAngelo."

"What's she got to do with this?" Hudson queried.

"Who knows a man better than his ex-wife," Blake said simply. I snapped my fingers in his direction.

"Exactly. If the pair of you can create a diversion to lure this Carla King off my back, it'll give me time to talk to Sally, and maybe even time to talk with your guys too. If I'm quick enough I can visit Tyson Lemar and Donnie The Face as well."

"Let me get this straight. You want your two protectors to deliberately abandon you so you can go and interview potential killers?" Blake said with a raised brow. Hudson had a similar expression.

"What, you think I can't look after myself?" I asked. "I stopped both of you in your tracks when you were having your throwdown. I can handle you, I can handle a couple of puny humans, right? Or are you saying these mobsters and boxers are tougher than the pair of you?"

"Not likely," Blake said firmly.

Hudson smiled. "Damn it, Wick, you're good at getting your way." He looked at Blake and the smile faltered. "I don't think the two of us can work together though."

"If you both want to keep being my protectors you're going to have to learn eventually." I stood up from the table, getting ready to go. "Come up with a diversion that'll keep Carla King occupied for an hour or two tomorrow. No fire, no explosions, and no fighting with each other. Is that clear?"

The two men stared at one another from across the table, looking thoroughly uncomfortable.

"Clear," Hudson murmured.

"As mud," Blake mumbled reluctantly.

"Good, then I'm going. Call me when you've come up with a plan. And remember, boys... play nice."

* * *

THE NEXT MORNING, I was up bright and early, ready for a day of sleuthing. I was prepared to clear my name; Carla King wasn't going to drag me through the papers anymore!

"Sheesh, looks like that King woman is really dragging you through the papers," Zelda said as she came into the kitchen holding the newspaper. "You seen this?" she said.

"I was lucky enough to get a sneak preview yesterday," I mumbled. "Anyway, that doesn't matter. I've got my own leads and I'm going to chase them down today!"

"You do?" Zelda asked in surprise.

"Uh-huh, I do. And I only want one thing out of you today, Zelda."

"I already told you last night, I grilled Celeste all morning about the Gordo thing. She wouldn't tell me anything!" Zelda protested. When I got back to the apartment yesterday, I was floating off the floor, excited to find out what Zelda had learned after working with Celeste all day. Zelda however had turned up nothing.

"Well you better find out something today, or I'm changing the locks!"

"This is my apartment!" Zelda laughed.

"Hermes, Phoebe, everything good with you guys?"

"Actually, I've got a few complaints—" Hermes began.

"Brilliant, and what about you, Phoebe? Anything you want to warn me about?"

"Pack an umbrella," she said sagely.

Hermes fake coughed. "Talking weather station," he said, coughing loudly again to 'cover' the words.

Glancing out the window I could see a crisp autumn day. "Phoebe, there isn't a cloud in the sky. It's not going to rain today!" The strange owl just blinked, her eyelids moving a little out of time with one another. "Okay then. Right, y'all. I'm off out for a day of productivity. Time to clear my name!"

As I skipped out of the apartment building and made my way to my van my phone started ringing. "Good morning, Hudson," I said, turning on the engine.

"Someone's in a good mood," he remarked.

"What can I say, I'm feeling strangely optimistic about today. Hopefully you're calling to tell me that you and Blake have come up with an awesome diversion."

"We have indeed, and guess what? No explosions, no fire, and no fistfights. In fact, I'd say me and old dog breath have been getting on quite well. Isn't that right, Blake?"

"You're treading on thin ice, freako!" Blake shouted in the background.

"Really sounds like it's going great," I said with a weak smile. "So what's the diversion?"

"Hey, give that back. I was talking—!" The sound of a struggle followed.

"Hey, Zora, Blake here. The diversion was actually my idea. I looked through some of Carla King's old articles and she *really* loves writing about men's swimming events. I rounded up the boys from the pack and set up a last-minute swimming race in the lake. She's taken the bait hook, line, and sinker. Carla King is currently on her way to the south side of the lake, and she'll be there for at least two hours."

"That's brilliant!" I said. "But what if she gets bored and comes back early?"

"Well, that's the brilliant part—" Blake began, but the sound of another struggle followed.

"I've got MAGE on standby to handle that part," Hudson said. "If King gets bored and turns around, I can have the guys at HQ create an artificial traffic jam. She'll be stuck here for hours."

"They can do that?" I said in surprise.

"Trust me, I could have King stuck on the south side of the lake until ten tonight if I wanted to. You've got all the time in the world. Do you want me to come back over and act as your backup? Blake might be at home staring at his half-naked 'bros' but it's not my idea of a good time."

"No, I'm fine," I laughed. "Just focus on getting along with one another. I appreciate this, really."

"The dog's not so bad. He just needed a leader to look up to, someone to show him some discipline—hey, get off, you're not having it back!" With that the phone call ended abruptly. I rolled my eyes. It still sounded like Blake and Hudson had their issues, but at least they were *sort of* getting on.

I put the address of Mark Mobson's ex-wife into my phone and pulled out onto the road. I had a few hours to investigate without anyone following me. I had to make the most of it.

CHAPTER 16

*S*ally DeAngelo's house was a large McMansion on the edge of the suburbs. I parked the van, walked up to the front door, and knocked. A moment later a tanned middle-aged woman in leopard print answered the door.

"Hi, I'm—" I began.

"I know who you are!" Sally said in an abrasive Jersey accent. Was everyone around here from Jersey? "You're the girl that snuffed Markie! I don't know if I should slap you or kiss you!"

"Kiss me?" I said, perplexed by the reaction.

"Well let's be honest, doll face. You've done a lot of people a favor by getting rid of that creep. Now what I don't understand is why you'd be here knocking on my door. If it's money you want then you can hit the sidewalk, honey. I ain't—"

"I don't want money; I just wanted to talk. Ten minutes of your time, that's all."

Sally thought about it briefly and then threw her hands in the air. "What the hell, I ain't got anything else going on this morning. What's your poison? Gin? Cosmo? Don't tell me, you're one of those book types. You don't drink."

"Usually not at this time in the morning," I said, laughing

nervously as Sally DeAngelo stepped aside to let me in. "A cup of tea will do me fine... my!" I said, stepping inside. "What a... *lovely* house you have here."

The entryway to Sally DeAngelo's house was *all* leopard print, and when I say *all*, I mean every conceivable surface. The stairs, the marble flooring, the faux-marble pillars, the wallpaper... even the crystals on the chandelier.

Sally shut the door. "The leopard is my spirit animal," she said. "That's what my shrink told me anyway. Follow me, kitchen is this way."

"Your shrink gave you a spirit animal?" I queried, following Sally into a kitchen that was also fully decked out in leopard print. I had no idea that leopard print fridges were a thing until now.

"Well, she's not so much a shrink; more a palm reader. But she didn't *give* me the spirit animal. It's always been inside me, you know, since I was born. She said I was a leopard in my past life." Sally set about making me a cup of tea while regaling me with stories of her past life as a leopard. I listened patiently for several minutes, smiling politely as the curious woman opened up to me.

Once the tea was done, she set the cup down in front of me and poured herself a martini. "Of course, I was the alpha female, you know, the leader of the pack. A lot of people don't know this about big cats, they assume the men give all the orders and the females do the work; it's actually the other way around. The women control everything. Just like real life."

"Hey, sisters are doing it for themselves," I said, taking a sip of my tea which was, of course, in a leopard print mug.

"So what did you want to talk about?" Sally asked, taking a seat at the breakfast bar and pulling out a leopard print cigarette. She lit it and took a long drag. "You come here to tell me why you killed him? To be honest, I don't care. He deserved it. What he do? Beat you up? Knock you up? All of the above?"

"Uh, none actually. I barely knew the guy. I'm guessing you've seen the video of him in my bakery?"

"No," Sally said, letting out another large plume of smoke. "But my daughter told me all about it. I try not to let Mark into my life too much these days. I don't care about his tragic little internet show. He came in and gave you a hard time, right? That's kind of his thing. Then you gave him some poisoned cupcake or whatever."

"That's what the police are saying." I filled Sally in on the missing details as best as I could, but I got the impression she wasn't really listening. Something told me this wasn't her first martini of the morning.

"Oh, so you really are maintaining this innocence thing, huh?" Sally winked and blew out more smoke. "Good for you, girl. I still don't understand why you're here though."

"I'm trying to clear my name," I said. "Is there anyone you could think of that might have good reason to harm Mark?"

Sally laughed, almost choking on her drink. "The list of people that don't have a reason would be much shorter, put it that way."

"No one at the top of that list though?" I asked.

"What are you, some kind of detective or something?" she asked.

"Not in any official capacity, though I helped solve my aunt's murder a few weeks ago."

"Ah… so you're one of those types," she said, tapping ash into a leopard print ashtray. "Honestly, honey, I've not been involved in Markie's life for a long time. He was a cheating parasite, and I'm good to be rid of him. I've got a new man now, and I'm doing much better for myself. I even tried to kill Mark a few times!"

"You what?" I said in surprise.

"Yeah." Sally laughed and took another drag. "Never serious though, just more a cry for attention type of thing. I shot at him, but always missed on purpose, you know, that type of thing."

"Right…" I said slowly, wondering if Sally should be on the suspect list.

"Listen, Zora, was it? I made my peace with Markie a long time ago. I mean I friggen' hate the guy and I wish I never met him, but he gave me two beautiful children. Some days I feel like shooting at them too, but they're good kids, and because of them I got to sucker alimony out of Markie boy every month. A pretty penny too; the county judge says it was a record amount for the state."

I turned my head. "So Mark legally had to give you a wad of money every month." I said the words out loud, but they were more for my own benefit as I processed the information.

"Yeah, it's income assessed, and back then Mark's brother was putting a lot of money into the club, so it looked like Mark was making big money."

"Wait, this is the football player, right? What's his name?" I asked.

"Who, Jerry? You don't know Jerry Mobson? All-star quarterback, two Superbowl wins?"

I stared blankly at her. "I'm not really much of a sports person."

Sally took another puff of her cigarette. "Honestly, sweetie, me neither, but it's a big part of the famiy as you can imagine. Poor Markie, bless his heart, always living in his brother's shadow—keen to make a name for himself, you know. Of course Jerry wanted to help him too, and he gave Markie the money, he gave him a lot of money, but…"

"But?" I prompted.

"Markie liked to think of himself as some maverick businessman, but even with his brother's investment his clubs were in the red most months. Jerry was basically pouring his money down the drain. He could never say no to Markie though… I still don't think he's cut him off to this day; that's the only way Markie keeps his clubs open."

"So on top of his failing clubs Mark had to pay you a hefty alimony every month. Did he always pay?"

"Oh, you betcha. Markie was terrified of the idea of going to prison. He acted tough, but he was a big softie really. So as much as I wanted to kill the guy, I much preferred the idea of letting that knife twist slowly every thirty days, hit him where it hurts, the money."

"So you literally had no reason to kill him," I surmised.

Sally laughed. "No reason? Doll face, I had plenty of reasons, but I had ten thousand more not to kill him every payday."

"Ten thousand a month? Geez," I said through a long whistle.

"Yah, and I think now you can scratch me off that little suspect list in your mind," she said. Sally stubbed her cigarette out in the ashtray and lit another one.

"You weren't on my list," I sputtered, not very convincingly.

"Zora, doll, I'm a housewife—do you know what kind of circles I run in? You practically have to be a mind reader in this world. All those skanks always plotting to dethrone me. It's insidious! You like that word? I got it from my word-a-day calendar."

"Nicely used," I said glumly, striking Sally's name off my mental list.

"Thanks. I don't take no offense by you suspecting me, of course; it's only natural. I watch those daytime crime procedurals. They give me life. Who else you eying up?"

"I uh... I don't know if I should be talking about this stuff with you."

"Oh, come on, it'll be fun! Bounce some ideas off me. I'm a pro!"

"This feels very strange, but okay. I wanted to try and talk with two more people today. Tyson Lemar—"

"The boxer?" Sally said, raising her brows. "What did Markie do to him?"

"His daughter," I answered. "Phoenix, she died of an overdose in one of his clubs."

Sally nodded her head very slowly as if recalling the memory. "I remember that now, tragic. Markie really was a scumbag, wasn't he? I don't know what I ever saw in him—you know he wasn't always like this; he used to be nice, quiet... anyway. Yeah, I could see Lemar having reason to kill Markie, but he's more of a fists kind of guy, no?"

"That remains to be seen, I guess," I said.

"Who else you got?"

"Some mob guy," I said, searching my phone for the notes. "Ah, there it is. Donnie The Face." I looked up as Sally burst out laughing. "What's... funny?" I asked.

"Oh, nothing!" she said, wiping tears from her eyes. "Damnit you're going to make my makeup run!" Sally fanned herself in attempt to still the tears. After a few deep breaths she composed herself.

"Okay, okay. I'll tell you. Phew. If you wanted to talk to Donnie you should have just said."

"You're friends with him?" I asked.

"Friends?!" Sally held up her hand, showing me a huge engagement ring on her finger. "Uh, sweetie, hello?! You're looking at the future Mrs. Donnie The Face! We're engaged to be married!"

"I…" My mouth flapped open and closed as I processed that unexpected turn. "I don't know what to say. Congratulations? Where can I find Donnie?"

"As luck has it, he's in the den, watching crappy old movies. That's kind of his thing. Come on; I'll go show you!"

* * *

I FOLLOWED Sally DeAngelo through her leopard print house, to a dark, medium-sized room that acted as a home theatre. Sally opened the door, a wedge of bright light cutting into the dark room. Even in the dim light I could see the pervasive leopard print everywhere.

"What took you so long?" a man said from one of the eight huge leather armchairs facing a small cinema screen on the wall. All the other chairs were empty, and an old black and white movie was playing. Turning around he saw me and paused the movie.

"Donnie, this is Zora Whip—"

"Wick," I corrected.

"Right, Zora Wick. She's asking questions about Markie."

"What are you, a cop?" Donnie said as he stood up and turned around properly. His face moved with recognition. "Sally, she's the girl that whacked Markie!"

"I didn't 'whack' anyone. Don't believe everything you read in the papers."

Donnie scoffed. "You're telling me? The amount of lies that rag has printed about me over the years, let me tell you."

"It's terrible," Sally added. "They said Donnie was a cold-blooded killer. He's a legitimate businessman!"

"Yeah… I'm sure," I said, eyeing up the large Italian American man that was clearly in the mob.

"Zora's trying to clear her name; she's some sort of investigator."

"Sounds like a cop to me. No disrespect, Miss Whip, but get the hell out of my house."

"It's Wick," I said through my teeth. "And I'm not a cop. I'm just trying to clear my name."

"She's cool, Donnie. Just answer her questions," Sally said, her tone becoming slightly sterner.

Donnie noticed the change in Sally's voice. He rolled his eyes and looked at me. "What exactly do you want to know?" he said. "That pig-faced moron got what was coming to him."

"Can you think of anyone that would have reason to hurt Mark?" I asked.

"Apart from you?" Donnie said, looking at me in a scrupulous fashion.

"Donnie," Sally said in a warning tone.

"Alright, don't get your leopard print in a twist," Donnie said, batting his hand at his fiancée. "What can I say, Mobson was gifted at making enemies. Lord knows I nearly killed the fella. I decided it wasn't worth it though. I let him live as a favor to Jerry."

"His older brother?" I asked.

"Of course, his older brother. Jerry is a local legend around here. Everyone knows it was Jerry's money going into Mark's pockets anyway. Mark was a nobody; not worth wasting your time on him."

"He slept with your wife," I said. A muscle started twitching in Donnie's eye.

"Yeah, he did, and you know what? I broke his hand for it. Pulled all my money out of the club after that too; never made a dime with that scumbag anyway. I had him pay me back everything he owed me, and then I set sail."

"Your divorce finalized this week, didn't it?" I said. "Some would say the timing looks suspicious."

Donnie narrowed his eyes at me. "I see, so you're trying to pin this thing on me, huh?"

"I'm just asking questions."

"Listen here, Miss Whip—"

"Wick."

"It's not my fault you decided to whack a guy and got all sloppy about it. You know what real men do? They take ownership of their mistakes, keep their mouths shut, and do the time. You're not pinning this on me, because I had nothing to do with it. I can even prove it!"

"How's that?" I asked.

Donnie lifted his right trouser leg, revealing a metal ankle collar with a flashing red light.

"House arrest," Sally said sadly. "He's got another two months in that bad boy."

"Judge says I was intimidating witnesses," Donnie said with a shrug. "I call it cement shoe negotiation. Difference of opinion."

"Donnie can't leave the house," Sally said. "Hasn't been out since September!"

"So, it couldn't have been you," I said in realization.

"Nope," Donnie said through a smarmy grin. "And to be honest I'd probably shake Markie's hand now if I saw him. Getting rid of my old lady was the best thing that ever happened to me. Sally's a pain in the butt, but she's a breath of fresh air!"

"Aw, Donnie!" Sally said, somehow taking that to be romantic.

"Are we done here?" Donnie said to me.

"Yeah…" I grumbled. "Thanks for your time."

Sally led me back to the front door of the house, stopping on the porch to talk a moment. "Sorry we couldn't be more help, Zara—"

"Zora."

"Oh, hey, you're a baker, right? Be a doll and give me a professional opinion. Wait right there!" Sally hurried off in the direction of the kitchen and came back a second later holding a plate with a brownie upon it. "Trying to perfect my brownie recipe. Try this. Tell me what you think. No lies!"

I picked up the brownie and had a small bite. It was pretty good. "Hey, it's not half bad, I—" I paused upon noticing something. "Are those white chocolate drops?"

"Yeah, little twist on an old classic. What do you think?"

I swallowed the brownie, wondering if I was about to drop dead from strychnine poisoning. The brownie that poisoned Mark Mobson had white chocolate drops in it too. "It's uh… good!" I said, putting the rest of the brownie back on the plate. Sally noticed my panic.

"Are you sure? Hey! Where are you going?!"

"I've… got somewhere to be. Bye!"

With that I started running for the van. If there was poison in that brownie I had to act.

Fast.

CHAPTER 17

I ran to the van, my whole body shaking as nerves consumed me. As soon as I was inside, I pulled out my phone and called Zelda.

"So guess who pulled a sickie this morning. Celeste left me to run the café alone. I don't have any answers about this Gordo—"

"Poisoned!" I shouted. "I think I've been poisoned! What do I do?!"

"What? Okay, wait a minute, let me think, where are you?!" Zelda said in one fast blur.

"Palmdale! What do I do? Is there a spell, can I—argh!" I screamed as a blue portal opened up in front of me, the figures of two familiar men spilling out, fighting with one another as they crashed to the tarmac.

It was Blake and Hudson. They both jumped to their feet. Blake ran to the door and opened it, scooping me into his arms.

"What is going on here?!" I said in alarm.

"If you've been poisoned, we need to act fast; we have to get the poison out of your system," Hudson said.

I gawped as Blake ran across the tarmac, heading straight for the blue portal that had appeared in front of the van. "Hurry up, hurry up!" Hudson shouted, waving his arms wildly for Blake to jump through the portal.

"I'm faster than you, idiot!" Blake shot back as he jumped through the portal.

One second we were on the street outside Sally DeAngelo's house. As Blake jumped through the portal we landed in a corridor with smooth black tiles and gray walls. Hudson jumped through behind us, and I saw the portal vanish.

"Which way?!" Blake shouted, spinning helplessly on the spot.

"Down here, follow me!" Hudson said, charging forward down the corridor.

"Can someone please tell me what's going on?!" I said, my words juddering with each one of Blake's heavy steps.

"She'd delirious!" Blake said. "We've got to be quick!"

"I am not delirious, you idiot. Just very confused!"

Hudson burst through a door at the end of the corridor, revealing a stark-white laboratory where a young Asian man in a lab coat was sitting at a desk with a pipette in his hand. He looked up, seemingly not expecting this intrusion.

"It's Zora, the Prismatic—" Hudson said quickly. "She's been poisoned."

"Get her on the bed now. What poison?" the doctor said as he set his equipment down quickly. Blake carried me over to a hospital bed in the corner and set me down.

"It's probably strychnine," I said. "One mouthful of brownie."

The young doctor gave me an unsure look. "When?"

"Uh… ninety seconds ago?" I hazarded. Everything had happened so fast it was hard to tell.

"Are you dizzy, out of breath? Having trouble with breathing?"

"I'm a little dizzy from whatever that portal was…" I said, looking at both Blake and Hudson. The pair of them were standing quietly behind the doctor, anxious expressions wrought on their faces.

"My name is Frank, but everyone calls me Yoshi—" the young doctor said.

"Is that your original name?" I asked.

"Nope, I'm just really good at Mario. I grew up in Idaho."

"Well I hope this poison *does* kill me, because I want to die now," I said, my cheeks blazing red with embarrassment.

"Don't worry about," Yoshi laughed, his hands moving quickly as he performed various tests with different sets of medical apparatus—I had no idea what any of it was. "This is going to hurt," he said, stabbing me with a small needle.

"Ah!" I said, yanking back my arm as he stabbed it.

"I *did* warn you," he laughed, turning over the needle and looking at a readout. "There's no human poison inside you. Your blood sugar is a little high. Let's have a look for magic…"

Yoshi threw his medical apparatus onto a silver tray besides him, grasped my head in his hands, and turned it so I was looking into his eyes.

"Hold on to something; you're probably going to be sick," he said.

"I—what?"

Without any warning it happened. It was as if I was strapped to a roller coaster, launching forward like a bullet from a gun. It felt like I shot forward right into his eyes, punching through a black veil and then suddenly finding myself in his mind, twisting and turning through the corridors of his brain at a million miles an hour.

It ended as quickly as it began, stopping once the young doctor took his hands off me. I turned and threw up over the side of the bed, where Blake just so happened to be standing with a bowl.

"Told you that'd happen," Yoshi said calmly, picking up a clipboard and marking something on it.

"Magic poison?" Blake asked. "Her body is expelling it?"

"No," Yoshi laughed. "The process for magical examination can be a little intense. It's the quickest way to do a full checkup though." Yoshi signed the clipboard and slipped it into the end of the bed. "Miss Wick, I'm happy to sign you off on a clean bill of health. No poison in your body."

"No poison?" Blake asked. Hudson also looked concerned.

"She's fit as a fiddle," Yoshi said. "Though your cortisol levels are a little high. Maybe dial back on the stress a tad."

145

Easier said than done.

"I don't understand," Hudson said.

"Well, that makes two of us," I said, sitting up properly in the bed. My head was spinning after Yoshi's magical examination, my temples pounding. "What the heck was that, guys? I was sitting in my van and then you both fall out of the sky!"

"Did you really think I was going to let you go hunting down a killer by yourself?" Hudson asked. "I've set up triggers to alert me if you're in danger. My systems picked up your elevated heartbeat, a rise in adrenaline, and the word 'poison'. As soon as it triggered, I had MAGE open up a portal to your location."

"He tried to get away without me," Blake pointed out. "But I made sure I was here too."

I stared at the pair of them in disbelief. "Is everyone in this town spying on me?"

"Uh, not spying," Hudson said, raising his hand. "It's a magical safeguard system that only notifies me if it thinks you're in trouble."

"That sounds like spying with extra steps," I said.

"Hey, it saved your life, didn't it?" Blake asked.

"So, you're taking his side now?" I remarked.

"I'm not taking anyone's side. Just saying, if you *had* been poisoned, we'd be heroes right now."

"To be fair you didn't really do much," Hudson said. "Just sort of got in the way."

Blake looked at Hudson with fury in eyes and clenched his fists. "Don't think I won't strike just because we're on your territory, you freak."

"Try it," Hudson smirked. "This is MAGE HQ. Make one wrong move and you'll be werewolf dust."

"I would strongly advise against any type of combat from either of you," Yoshi interjected. "The defense systems here are extremely precise. I don't want any blood in my laboratory."

"Wait, we're at MAGE HQ now?" I asked Hudson. "I thought you said this was a top-secret facility."

"It is, but I also knew it was the only place you could get healed quickly enough if you were poisoned. Besides, you're in the building, but you don't know *where* the building is."

"That's a good point…" I murmured.

"I know where we are," Blake said. "My sense of direction is impeccable. We're near the old flour factory."

"Swing and a miss," Hudson said. "Don't worry, you won't even remember this trip once we're out. Neither of you will."

"What does that mean?" I asked. "There aren't any windows. I can't tell where we are anyway."

"Doesn't matter, we don't take any chances. The building is protected with intense magical systems," Hudson said. "If you're not on the list your memory will be blanked. Just the trip here of course. Now, can you tell us what happened?"

"I uh… man, where do I begin?" I recalled my visit to Sally DeAngelo, and that Donnie The Face had been there too, ending the story as I took a bite of her brownie.

"I don't understand," Blake said. "Why did you think you'd been poisoned?"

"Because her brownie had white chocolate drops in it, just like the one that killed Mark Mobson." Both Hudson and Blake raised their brows in intrigue.

"There's got to be more than one person out there that puts white chocolate drops in their brownies," Blake suggested.

"I don't know, it's not super common, and what are the odds? Anyway, as soon as I saw those chocolate drops, I thought I'd been poisoned. I guess I just started freaking out. I called Zelda for help, but then you guys showed up. Oh man, Zelda!" I grabbed at my pocket for my phone, but it wasn't there, I must have left it back in the van. "She's going to be freaking out!"

Yoshi stepped forward. "Well, you're good to go, Miss Wick. All looks good here."

"Thanks, Yoshi," Hudson said. "I appreciate it."

"Don't mention it. Still on for poker night this weekend?"

"Are you kidding? You guys wipe me out every time. I might have to pass."

We left the laboratory and walked back down the hall. I half-expected another portal to open up in the corridor, but when I blinked, I found myself standing on the street outside my van—it was like a passage of time had vanished.

Blake flinched. "What the hell? How did we get here?!"

"Calm down, you idiot, I told you the system would blank your minds," Hudson said.

"How did we get here?" I asked.

"You're not surprised to see me?" he asked.

"Why would I be surprised to see you? We were literally just at MAGE together," I said.

A grave expression came over Hudson's face. "Wait, you remember that?"

"Well, we were just leaving. Walking down the corridor and poof—now we're here."

"Hm, looks like the system didn't erase as much from your mind. It penetrates easier on simpler brains. You're a Prismatic Witch, so it figures you resisted it a little."

"Can someone please explain what's going on?!" Blake shouted. "One minute we're at the lake, now we're here!"

"You can deal with that," I said to Hudson.

"Where are you going?" he asked.

"I have another suspect to interview." I climbed into my van and noticed my phone was ringing. I had thirty-four missed calls, all from Zelda. I answered the phone.

"Where are you?!" she panicked. "I'm coming now!"

"I'm fine," I said. "It was a false alarm. Sorry."

"I'll be there in five—wait, you're fine?"

"Yeah, sorry. False alarm. Everything is okay. It wasn't poison."

There was a long moment of silence before Zelda responded. "You know there are some days when I hate being your sister."

"Full human experience, am I right?" I laughed awkwardly. "Sorry, seriously. I'll make it up to you later and we can go out for dinner. Sound good?"

"Maybe," she grumbled. "But you're paying. And we're having dessert."

"It's a deal. See you later, sis." I ended the call, started the engine, and wound down the window to address Hudson again.

"You're sure you're okay?" he asked me.

"Yeah, I'm fine. Just take Blake and get back to the lake. We need to make sure Carla King doesn't come snooping back to town."

"Seriously, can someone tell me what's going on?" Blake said, still reeling from the mind-blanking. Hudson rolled his eyes, looked up to the heavens, and let out a loud sigh.

"How did I get lumped with this idiot?" he groaned.

"Play nice, remember. I've got a boxer to grill. I'll call if I need you." With that I pulled away from the curb and onto the road. Time to interview a violent boxer, no big deal.

CHAPTER 18

*T*yson Lemar's boxing gym was situated in a small industrial lot, next to the lake on the eastern edge of town. Several large warehouses all faced off next to another, men driving forklift trucks, large containers of fresh-caught fish glistening under the sun. I parked the van and saw a group of dock workers smoking cigarettes and playing poker on an upturned crate.

It was like I'd walked into machismo central.

The boxing gym was a square building made of red brick, it's entrance a simple corrugated loading door that was currently up to the ceiling. As I approached, I could see the entirety of the gym's interior, a full-sized boxing ring where two men were sparring, surrounded by gym equipment and punching bags—all being used by the other dozen men in there.

I walked past the reception desk, which was a piece of plywood stacked on some cinderblocks. Sitting there was an obese man with a receding hairline and a fat golden chain around his neck. He was wearing a string vest, smoking a cigar, and reading a nude magazine.

"Let me guess," he said without looking up. His voice was thick and gravelly. "You want to learn how to defend yourself. Well you came to the right place. My papa, he told me to marry a woman that can throw a punch. What is it, boyfriend knocking you around? Media got you scared? Let me tell you, you can't believe everything you see on the news, why just the other day—"

"I'm not looking to fight," I said, wondering if I had a sign on me somewhere that said, 'Talkative people, come and have it'.

The man looked at me in an unsure way and tilted his head from side to side. "You sure? Your arms are pretty scrawny. Not a lot of meat on you. If someone came at you in a dark alley—"

"Then they'd regret it," I said. "Trust me, I can defend myself." Before owning a wand I'd not really believed that as much, but since becoming a witch I felt a lot safer going out into the world. I had a literal bang stick in my pocket.

"Alright, suit yourself," he said, chewing on his cigar a little. "What you here for then? Picking up fellas? Save your time. You're looking at a warehouse full of degenerates."

"I'm looking for Tyson Lemar," I said. "I'd like to talk to him."

The big guy snorted. "Lemar's a busy man. Do you have an appointment?"

"No, not really. It's concerning Mark Mobson."

"You a reporter?" the man said through narrow eyes.

"Nope, just a woman trying to clear her name." With that sentence it was like a bell rang in the big guy's mind. His eyes opened wide and he stood up straight. "Wait, it's you!"

"Oh god," I muttered to myself, wondering what was coming next.

"You're the broad that poisoned that jabronie! Man, you weren't kidding when you said you can defend yourself. I'll get Mr. Lemar now. He's been talking you up for the last two days!"

"I didn't poison the guy—" I began, but the big man had already taken off into the gym. He didn't go far; he rushed over to a figure that was coaching someone on the other side of the ring. He looked over at me immediately—it was Tyson Lemar.

Lemar and the big man quickly walked over to the desk. Tyson Lemar pulled off his training equipment and held out his hand, his eyes glimmering with approval. He was a big man, just over six feet tall and all muscle. His black skin glistened under the warehouse lighting.

"Lemar," he said, shaking my hand gently. "Tyson Lemar. I don't know to what I owe the honor, but it is a damned pleasure to meet you."

"I'm guessing you saw my name in the paper—" I said.

"Are you kidding me? It's all anyone has been talking about. You're a hero in my book. Heck, you're a VIP guest at Lemar Boxing Gym, you hear that? Free membership for life!"

"That's very flattering," I said, "but I didn't actually—"

"I don't know who told you to come here, but I'm guessing you heard about what that scumbag did to my Phoenix." Tyson's jaw steeled, his eyes watering slightly. He looked at the big man in the string vest. "Sal here will tell you; it almost broke me. When I heard what that rat did to my baby girl, I nearly killed him. Heck—I would have if his goons didn't pull me off him."

"I didn't kill him," I said. "It's just conjecture. The papers want a villain, and they picked me."

The look of approval in Tyson's eye dimmed somewhat. After a moment his smile faded too. "You're telling the truth."

"I am," I said, nodding reluctantly. "I barely knew the guy; I've just been framed for his murder."

"That's a damn shame," Tyson said. "I guess that still leaves the question as to what you're doing here."

"I'm trying to find out who did kill him. You knew Mark Mobson. Any idea who might have wanted him dead? And before you say it, I know he had a lot of enemies."

"Then it sounds like you've already done your research. Listen, I don't know who got him—I honestly thought it was you. Whoever it was, I want to know so I can shake their hand."

"You had more than enough reason to want him dead," I pointed out.

"I did want him dead, and I'm glad he is." Tyson stared at me for a moment and then added, "But I didn't kill the guy. That's what you're getting at here, isn't it?"

"I'm just trying to explore all the options here," I said, holding the gaze of the man that was much larger than me.

Tyson Lemar pulled a phone out of his pocket. "You know, if you're going to do the whole amateur investigator thing you might want to get better at doing your homework," Tyson said as he turned his phone around to show me something.

"What's that supposed to mean?" I asked as a video started playing. In it I saw Tyson standing ringside at a busy match.

"I've been in Vegas for the last week; one of my boys had an exhibition fight. I just got back last night. My flight came in late," he explained. "So…"

"So, you couldn't have killed Mark Mobson," I summarized. Another suspect bit the dust.

"So, I couldn't have killed him," he repeated. "But understand this, I broke out the champagne when I heard the news. Heck, I'm a little disappointed it wasn't you. I really thought I'd met one of my heroes today."

"What makes you so sure I didn't do it?" I asked.

"If I'm being honest, the details seemed a little sketchy to me. You knew that moron was streaming his interaction with you. It doesn't make a whole lot of sense to serve a guy a poisoned brownie when you've got an audience. It makes even less sense when you consider the interaction is free to watch on the internet after the fact."

"My thoughts exactly," I said. "You really have no idea who else could have done this?"

"They say poison is a woman's weapon, but maybe that's just a cliché."

"From the looks of things, every woman that ever met Mark Mobson hated the guy, so that doesn't narrow it down," I muttered.

"You really think you can catch this guy?" Tyson Lemar asked me.

"To be honest I don't know. I've done it once before, but that was sort of a fluke. I had a few avenues of thought, but as of this moment they're all closed."

"That's a shame. Well, Miss Wick, if you'll excuse me, I've got training to get back to. Let me know if you catch the person that did kill Mobson. I want to shake their hand."

With that disappointing interaction done I left the boxing gym and made my way back to the van.

As soon as I climbed in and closed the door a voice piped up behind my seat, scaring the life out of me. "How did it go then?"

"Argh!" I screamed, turning around and clutching my wand to defend myself against my attacker. I froze upon seeing Hermes and I lowered my wand. "What in the heck are you doing in here?" I said, putting the wand away.

"What are you talking about? I've been in here all morning. I thought you'd want a little company today seeing as Zelda was back in the café again." Hermes licked the back of his paw and started grooming his ears.

"Are you kidding me? I had no idea you were in here."

"Yeah, there's a chance I fell asleep, but I'm awake now!" he said cheerily. "Let's go interview some suspects!"

I stared at Hermes in disbelief. "Dude, I already interviewed everyone."

"Get out of town!" he said. "What? How long was I asleep?"

"I set off like two hours ago, so I'm guessing the entire time. I spoke with Mark Mobson's ex-wife, Donnie The Face, thought I got poisoned and was emergency evacuated to MAGE HQ by Hudson and Blake. It was a false alarm; then I came here."

"Huh," Hermes said, licking his paw again. "Seems like I missed quite a lot."

"Yeah… I was on the phone in here screaming to Zelda about being poisoned. How did you sleep through that?"

Hermes shrugged, if a cat *can* shrug. "I've always been a pretty solid sleeper. I try and get the recommended sixteen hours."

"Pretty sure eight hours is the recommended amount."

"For a *human* maybe. We cats are supposed to get a solid twelve to sixteen hours, though sometimes sixteen can leave me feeling a little grouchy. Some days I don't even wake up; I just sleep right through!"

"That I can imagine," I said with a laugh.

"So are you any closer to figuring out who murdered this guy?" Hermes asked, pouncing onto the passenger seat.

"Hm, no. Of the three main suspects they all have pretty tight alibis. Mark's ex-wife, Sally DeAngelo, was receiving a pretty hefty alimony payment. Donnie The Face has been under house arrest, and Tyson Lemar was in Vegas."

"Huh, sure doesn't look good for you, eh?" Hermes asked.

"No, it doesn't," I said as I started the van and pulled away from the lot. A few minutes later I was back on the other side of town. I parked up outside Zelda's apartment and climbed out of the van. As I did so a large black SUV pulled up behind me, a huge muscle-bound man climbing out. He was wearing shades, a cap, and a long black jacket, like he was trying hard to not be noticed. It started to rain, and I lamented the fact that I hadn't brought an umbrella. *Should have listened to Phoebe.*

My first instinct was caution. I didn't pull my wand out because the guy felt distinctly non-magical, but I wanted to be safe. "Can I help you?" I asked.

"You're Zora Wick, right?" he said.

"I am she," I said, wondering why this guy felt oddly familiar. "Do I know you from somewhere?"

The man slipped his shades down and I did recognize his eyes. I didn't know him, but I'd seen his face before; his brother had been in my café only a few days ago. "You're the football player."

He smiled awkwardly. "That's me. I'm Jerry, Jerry Mobson."

I froze in my tracks, the familiarity suddenly feeling sinister. This was the professional football player and older brother of Mark Mobson. "Uh, listen, I don't know what you read in the paper, but I did *not* kill your brother." I glanced back at Hermes on the sidewalk, giving him a silent look that meant *get ready, this could get ugly.*

"Relax," Jerry said with assurance. "I'm not looking for a fight. I actually came here to ask for your help. For what it's worth I don't think you're the killer either."

"You don't?" I asked.

He shook his head. "No, but I think someone is trying to frame you. I want you to help me figure out who's behind this. I did see you in the paper, but the story from a few weeks ago. You helped solve an old cold case, right?"

"My aunt's murder, that's correct." I paused and looked at Jerry, trying to get a measure on him. "I don't understand. Why would you approach your brother's suspected killer and ask them for help?"

Jerry laughed, acknowledging this bizarre situation. "I know it's unconventional, but there aren't any other investigators in this town, and you seem to have a knack for this sort of thing."

"What makes you so sure I'm innocent?" I asked.

"You just don't strike me as a killer. The whole thing doesn't make sense. You knew Mark was recording you. Why would you try and poison someone and let them record it on tape?" Jerry proffered.

"That's what I keep saying, but still... do you have any idea who would want your brother dead?"

"It was a long list, but I'd guess it has something to do with money. Mark was bad with money, and he was in debt."

"You think the mob had something to do with this?"

Jerry screwed his face up. "I... don't think so. If the mob want to kill someone they just up and do it. None of this poison business. That's not how they work."

"It seemed uncharacteristic to me too. I heard a lot of Mark's money came from you," I said. "Did you ever cut him off?"

"Not fully, though I guess I should have at one point. I think I was worried about him; I knew he was in trouble. I should have ripped the band-aid off a long time ago and just cut the money. I was still supporting him, though nothing like in the old days," Jerry admitted. "A lot of people think my funds are endless because I played professional football."

"Isn't that the case?" I asked.

"Don't get me wrong, I made a lot of money in my career, but once you reach the top your relationship with money and the people around you changes. I bought a house for just about every member of my extended family, I've got aunts and uncles and cousins that rely on me for financial assistance. I'm too old to play football now, and I'm doing just about every gig I can to keep the money coming in."

Taking a closer look, I realized Jerry's appearance was a little rough around the edges. His SUV was scuffed and dirty, his clothes looked like they were overdue a clean, and even his shoes—sneakers— looked like a small dog had been at them.

"Look, I've already been digging into Mark and his laundry list of enemies, but so far I'm just hitting dead end after dead end. I'm not sure how much help I can be," I admitted.

"I might just be able to help with that," Jerry said. "Providing you think you can help. I want justice for Mark. I know he wasn't a good guy, but he didn't deserve to die like that." He looked around the street as though to check no one was listening in on the conversation. We were currently the only ones out here. "I have a lead that can help."

"I'm listening," I said.

"Mark has a safe in his apartment, over on Ortega Heights. It's the Avalon building."

"That's the fancy building, right? I've driven past there a few times."

"Yeah, stacked to the brim with folk that have too much money and not enough sense." He looked at me, and I got the sense he worried about being hypocritical. "Look, I know I've done well for myself, but I grew up poor—I'm talking about people that have had everything handed to them."

"I get it. So, what about this safe? What's inside?"

"That's just it. I don't know, but I know Mark stored his most important items in there. Business contracts, blackmail, you get the idea. I don't know who killed Mark, but I think the inside of that safe might hold a few clues."

"So go and look in it?" I suggested.

"You don't think I tried? The security in the building is airtight. They won't let anyone in without Mark. I tried explaining the situation, but they don't give a damn. I can't exactly go back there and sneak in either. I don't exactly blend in."

"That's fair," I said. "So, what do you want me to do? Break into this apartment and crack the safe? I'm a baker, Mr. Mobson, not a professional thief."

"I've got a combination for the safe—1108—Mark used the same code for everything. As for getting into the apartment, I don't have an answer for that, but you're a resourceful young girl. I'm sure you can figure it out."

"I don't know about this…" I said unsurely.

"I'll take it that's a yes then?" Jerry Mobson asked.

On the one hand I didn't really have much choice. If I sat on my hands and did nothing I'd almost certainly go down as Mark's killer. Every other avenue had been a dead end so far, and this was my only remaining lead.

"I'll think about it," I said reluctantly. Jerry nodded, seemingly satisfied with the answer. "I'm staying at the Palm Hotel if you need me. *Elias Smith.* Let me know what you decide to do."

With that Jerry got back in his SUV and drove away. I made my way into Zelda's apartment, Hermes trotting at my side.

"For a minute I thought I would have to unleash some cat-fu on that guy!" Hermes said excitedly as we walked up the stairs.

"Yeah, I wondered the same thing myself."

"So what are you going to do?" he asked me. "Are you really going to break into this guy's apartment?"

I sighed. "I don't know, but one thing is for sure, I really don't have a lot of options left."

CHAPTER 19

"*J*f I had to summarize this plan in one word it would be...
bad idea," Zelda said as she watched me get ready for my
midnight excursion.

"Uh, that's two words, and I don't remember asking for your opinion," I fired back, lacing up my sneakers and pulling on a black hoodie.
I was wearing black leggings, to accompany the rest of my outfit. If I
was going to break in somewhere I figured I should at least try and
look like a burglar.

"I'm your sister. I get to stuff my unsolicited opinion down your
ear whenever I like. What if the police catch you breaking into this
guy's place? What if the press catch you?! That Carla King will have a
field day!" Zelda protested.

"Good thing they're not going to catch me then. I've already
broken into one place, and I didn't get caught then," I pointed out.

"Uh, you mean the time that someone shot at you with a gun?
Hardly a clean track record."

"Still—I know what I'm doing. This isn't my first rodeo; it's my...
second. And everyone knows the second rodeo is the best one—or
something. You're welcome to tag along and be my partner in crime."

Zelda just laughed. "Hard pass. I'm wondering if I should call

Hudson and Blake and get them to stop you. What do they think about all this?"

"They don't know anything about it, and they don't need to either. What they don't know can't hurt them. Besides, you don't have a way of getting in touch with them!"

Zelda pouted upon me pointing out that fatal flaw. "Argh, you called my bluff. Look, I really don't think you should go, but beyond me physically stopping you from leaving this apartment there's not much I can do about it."

"And I'd totally win in that fight," I pointed out. "You've got all the muscle of an anemic kitten."

"Do not!" she said. "I can look after myself!"

"Yeah, of course you can," I said, placating her. "Anyway, I'll be back in an hour. Gonna go and solve this murder."

I left the apartment—Zelda still chastising me all the while as I closed the door and headed for the stairs. Once I was on the ground floor I headed for the rear parking lot to get the van and saw Blake standing in front of me.

"Seriously?" I said, stopping in my tracks. "Shouldn't you be running around in the woods with your shirt off or something?"

"Funny," he said with an unamused smirk. "I'm here to stop you from doing something stupid."

"And how would you know I'm going to do something stupid?" I asked.

"Oh, just a funny feeling I had," he said.

"Let me guess, spying on me again? Really, this is starting to get old."

"Close but no cigar..." Blake said. He pulled out his phone so I could see the screen. According to his phone, *my* phone was currently engaged in a call with Blake. I grabbed my own phone out of my pocket and realized I had pocket-dialed him by accident, almost fifteen minutes ago. "I uh..." I began.

"You butt-dialed me," he said. "Pretty much broadcast your whole secret plan, not that I wouldn't have seen you sneaking out of the apartment at this hour of course. Your sister is right; this is a really stupid plan. Sneaking into the apartment of the person that everyone thinks you killed? You realize nothing about that looks good."

"Doesn't look much worse than me sitting in jail for a crime I didn't commit," I retaliated. "Someone is trying to frame me; I have to figure out who and *why*. There's a safe in Mark's apartment, and it might have the answers I need."

"Yeah, it might, and it might just be where the guy hides his weird sex toys. You have no idea what's in that thing." Blake rolled his neck on his shoulders. "Come on, let's get you back to your apartment. We'll find another way to clear your name." Blake took a step towards me, and I held my hand out.

"Take one more step and I'll zap you to the cruising altitude of a commercial airliner," I warned.

Blake laughed but looked a little nervous. "You can't do that. Right?"

"You want to find out?" I said, trying to sound serious and threatening at the same time. I couldn't actually fling him into the sky of course—right now my most dangerous magic consisted of baseball-sized projectiles that were invisible to the human eye—but Blake didn't have to know that.

He took a step back, easing off on his advance. "Alright, so what do you want to do?"

"I'm going to check out this apartment. You're welcome to come with me if you want. Something tells me you're only going to follow me anyway."

Blake thought about it for a moment and sighed. "Fine, but if anything seems off, the plan is toast."

"Agreed," I said, unlocking the van and climbing in via the driver-side door. Blake climbed in on the other side, the van tilting slightly at the unequal weight distribution. I fired up the engine, reversed out of the spot, and pulled onto the road. After a few minutes of quiet driving I felt the need to fill the silence.

"How was your day out on the lake with Hudson?" I asked.

"Not exactly in the top ten days of my life, put it that way," he murmured.

"What? I thought you would have enjoyed getting in a little bit of quality time with a guy you hate for absolutely no reason," I said sarcastically.

"I have my reasons," Blake said cryptically. "You know there's something off about that guy, right? He's not magical at all, he's as mortal as they come, but he can almost move at the same speed as me, and his strength isn't far off mine either. That shouldn't be possible for a human."

I had to hold back a smile as Blake profiled his archnemesis. From the fight I'd witnessed I'd say they were both equally matched, but Blake still wouldn't admit it out loud. "Probably one of the perks for working with MAGE. They're a mysterious spooky organization, right? Maybe they gave him some powers as a reward."

"That's exactly why I don't trust him. We know nothing about him, or what he's capable of. And MAGE is hardly any better."

"I know nothing about you either," I pointed out.

"My family has been protecting yours for generations. We took an oath to protect the arch witch in Compass Cove at all times, and it just so happens that always turns out to be a Wick witch. I'd say my resume is fairly ironclad. Freak boy on the other hand... there's something about him I don't like."

"Well, it sounds like the two of you got along well enough today, so thanks for that. It *did* make my life easier. Really. If you're both insisting on being my 'guardian' or whatever you want to call it then things go a lot smoother when you aren't fighting."

"I suppose so," he conceded quietly. "I'm not making any promises though, Zora. If he so much as looks at you the wrong way—"

"Yeah, yeah, I get it. You'll rip off your shirt and have another one of your macho fights. You know I'd almost guess you have a crush on the guy, seeing how willing you are to go skins and rub up against one another."

Something unexpected actually happened then; Blake cracked a smile. "Alright, quit it."

"Woah, did I penetrate the icy exterior of the wolf warrior?" I said, turning the van onto Compass Cove's main street. "I think I've earned a brownie point tonight. Where is Hudson anyway? I figured my second stalker would have been right behind you."

Blake shrugged. "I don't know, probably out putting pixies in handcuffs, or whatever pointless thing it is those MAGE guys do. Let's talk about something else, I'm done talking about Hudson," Blake said. "You said that the interviews today were a wash?"

"Yeah, pretty much." I'd already briefly recapped the day's findings to Blake and Hudson via text, but I went over it all again with Blake anyway just to pass the time.

"Sounds like they all had pretty good alibis," Blake pointed out. "Donnie under house arrest, Tyson not even in town. The only one that potentially could have done it is the ex-wife, what was her name, Sally?"

I nodded. "Yeah, but she was getting a five-figure alimony settlement off Mark every month. Doesn't make sense to slaughter that cash cow."

"That it doesn't..." Blake mused. "But you think the brownie she made was the same that killed Mark; *that's* pretty damning."

"Yeah, I have no idea what to think. Here's hoping the safe in his apartment holds some sort of clues." A few minutes later we pulled up in an alleyway a few streets away from Ortega Heights. "Alright, I'm going to hop out and make my way over to Mark's apartment building. Are you staying here?"

Blake shook his head. "I'll head to the rooftops and keep an eye on things from above. Here take this," he said, handing me a small black earpiece.

"What's this?" I asked.

"This'll let us communicate with one another. Just hold your finger to the piece to transmit a message."

"Fancy," I remarked, putting the piece into my ear. I checked my reflection in the rearview mirror and the earpiece was barely visible. The two of us got out of the van.

"What's your plan?" he asked me.

"I stole this from Zelda's room," I said, pulling a small magic book from my black backpack. "I skimmed through it. There are a few simple spells in here that can help me."

Blake eyed the book unsurely. "You're sure you're ready for spells like that?"

"I'm a pro," I said, shrugging off the uncertainty in his question. "Trust me, it'll be fine. A quick invisibility spell and I'll be in and out in a flash."

"If you say so," he said. "Don't drag it out. The quicker this is over the better."

"Agreed."

Without another word Blake vaulted up to a nearby rooftop with one effortless jump. I stared in amazement, blinking as he disappeared. His voice was in my ear a second later. "Am I coming in clear?" he asked.

"Yeah," I said, holding my finger on the earpiece to talk as I walked towards the street. "You ever thought about competing in the Olympics? You'd clean up!"

Blake laughed. "Pretty sure magic folk aren't supposed to take part in human sports. There's Olympics for paranormal folk, though I can't say I'm interested."

"Paranormal Olympics?" I asked. "Now *that* sounds interesting."

"Keep your eyes forward and focus on the plan," Blake said, killing the conversation. "It's time to get serious."

I mouthed his last words—*time to get serious!*—to myself silently, making a childish face as I did so. Before I reached the street I paused at the entrance to the alleyway and opened the book stolen from Zelda's room. It was small, not much bigger than the palm of my hand, and its red cover was faded and worn. Peeling gold letters made up the title, *Aga Bizva's Advanced Spells Made Easy – 45th edition*.

I flicked to the index page, which had the spells sorted alphabetically. *Animal Form, Clairvoyance, Frost Hands, Gust of Wind*, were among some of the spells my eyes moved over. I flicked straight to the spells starting with 'I' however, as I'd already found the spell I wanted to use. I found the corresponding page and reread through the spell.

Invisibility.

This simple spell is deceptively powerful, typically only requiring a third of one's daily magical reserves. If performed correctly the spell should grant the caster fifteen minutes of invisibility. To cast follow the wand diagrams below, repeating the phrase 'Visus ad Sanam'.

"Sounds easy enough," I said to myself, pulling my wand out from my magical aura. The aura was effectively an invisible pocket that surrounded my entire body. Most witches just used them to store their wands.

I went through the motions of the spell, repeating the phrase to myself while following the wand diagrams. As I started moving my wand, golden paths of light appeared in the air, and I realized I had to trace my tip along them. It was almost like I was playing some sort of rhythm-based dance game—pretty fun actually.

As I finished the last wand flourish, I felt the wand activate with a distinct poof of air. I heard a high-pitched bell ring in my mind and, looking down, I could no longer see my hands, or any of my body in fact. "Woah, I'm like… totally invisible!" I whispered to myself.

I was just about to close the book when I realized another line of words were appearing at the bottom of the spell, the ink slowly forming on the page. *Footnote: This rather amazing invisibility spell does have one small side effect. Every sound you make will be ten times louder.*

"Oh, for the love of—" I began. Blake's voice appeared in my ear, cutting me off.

"Zora? What's going on down there? I can't see you anywhere."

"I'm just getting ripped off by this prankster spell book," I said. "I've made myself invisible, and after I finished the spell this footnote appeared out of nowhere, warning me that any sound I make will be ten times louder!"

"Will you reign it in a little bit?" Blake said. "You nearly blew my eardrums. No need to shout!"

"I wasn't shouting, I was—" I then realized the spell was amplifying my voice, to the point where it sounded like I was shouting. I dropped my voice to a whisper. "Ah… crap. Is that better?"

"A little, you're still super loud though. I think you should keep your lips sealed until you're in the apartment."

"Good idea. I've got fifteen minutes of invisibility. I'll get moving."

I tucked the cursed spell book back into my bag and started hustling down the sidewalk towards the hotel. Even though I was trying to move quietly I could hear my feet quite easily, it sounded like I was seriously stomping on the ground.

As luck would have it a woman came out onto the sidewalk as I reached the building. I slipped through the automatic doors and stepped inside the bright lobby, eyeing up the guard sitting behind the desk on the opposite side of the room. I felt self-conscious of my breathing. Even though I was breathing normally it sounded like I'd just run a marathon. The guard looked up from his desk, eyeing the empty spot where I was standing.

"Someone there?" he said, getting up from the desk.

Stupid book, stupid book, stupid book!

The guard walked around the desk and came about halfway to the door, eyeing the plants in the corners as though someone was hiding behind them. He put a finger in his ear and wiggled it, like he was trying to get out some troublesome wax.

"Damn it, Bill, you're losing it," he muttered to himself. "You've got to get off these night shifts." The guard walked back to his desk, and I took another step forward. Even though I was trying to tread as cautiously as possible the soles of my shoes squeaked loudly across the quiet foyer.

Once again, the guard, who was still walking back to the desk, whipped his head around and looked right where I was standing. I was so petrified I was holding my breath now, terrified of making even the smallest sound. He started in my direction again, this time heading right for me.

If I didn't move, he was going to walk right into me, but if I moved again, he'd definitely know someone was there.

This was harder than I thought it would be.

CHAPTER 20

*P*anic consuming me, I stood there frozen, the guard only a few steps away until he'd collide with me. *Think, Zora, think!*

"Alright, who's there? Stop messing around!" the guard said as he charged forward. That's when I noticed a comically large buckle on his belt. In the center of it there was an eagle with outspread wings, the words 'Texas Ranger' surrounding it.

With no other ideas I panicked and pointed my finger at the buckle, willing my magic to do something, *anything!* A zing of invisible magic pinged out of my fingertip. The guard's belt unbuckled itself and his trousers dropped to the floor, tripping him over mid-stride.

I had to jump out of the way as the guard tumbled forward and hit the floor. My little jump made a large noise, but luckily it overlapped with the sound of the guard hitting the floor.

"What the?!" he shouted, scrambling to his feet and pulling his trousers up again. That's when the phone behind his desk started ringing. The guard muttered something to himself about ghosts and ran back to the desk to grab the phone.

"Good evening, you're through to the Avalon," he answered,

slightly out of breath. "Outside, right now?!" The guard placed the phone down and jogged out of the lobby via the front. Realizing this was my chance I kicked off my shoes, held them in my hands, and slid across the marble flooring in my socks, moving like I was walking over snow. I reached the elevator, zipped inside, and hit the button for Mark's floor, breathing a sigh of relief as the door's closed.

"My call worked then? Something told me you needed a little help," Blake's voice said, appearing in my ear.

"How could you tell?" I asked.

"That guard was awfully interested in that empty spot of air by the front door, and I could hear you up from the roof on the other side of the street."

"Am I *that* loud?!"

"Definitely louder than usual. I'm a shifter though, so I've got a heightened sense of hearing. Keep that in mind."

"So that was you on the phone? What did you say?"

"I put on a snooty voice and pretended to be one of the residents. Said I could see some kids outside spraying graffiti on the walls."

"It worked, good job. Quick thinking. I'm not sure I would have got past that guy without you!" The elevator doors dinged open, and I stepped out into the corridor. Thankfully there was no one else around, so I didn't have to worry about sneaking around. I followed the signs for Mark's door, finding it a few seconds later at the end of the corridor.

"I'm at the room," I said. "Now I just have to get inside."

"Please don't tell me you're going to use more spells from that book," Blake said.

"Ha, no, I've learned my lesson on that one," I replied, trying to keep my voice as a low whisper. "Luckily I've picked a few locks with magic already. This one should be easy. Let me focus on getting the door open."

I pulled out my wand again and willed *Helping Hand*, a magical hand that appeared at the end of my wand. It could pass through objects, but also manipulate things if I focused hard enough. I made the hand pass through the door and felt around for the lock on the other side. I couldn't see so I was aimlessly searching a little, but then I found it.

I had the hand grab the lock and twisted my wand. The lock clicked and the door opened. *Oh yeah, still got it!*

Very quietly I slipped inside the apartment and closed the door behind me. I muttered a quick spell, and a beam of light came out of the wand tip, revealing a luxury apartment that was bright and spacious.

"Wow, Mobson knew how to live," I said, holding one finger against the earpiece so I could communicate with Blake.

"Let me guess. Lots of white, lots of sharp angles, and not a lot of furniture."

"How did you know?" I asked.

"These rich guys are all the same," he muttered.

"It's a stark difference from your place," I said, recalling the dusty cabin stacked with cardboard boxes.

"Uh, I've only just moved in there, and besides, I'd take a cabin over some high-end condo any day. I'm happier out in the sticks."

"I think I agree," I said, moving forward into the apartment. "Feels devoid of personality in here." I stopped by the floor-to-ceiling windows that looked out over Compass Cove. "Can't complain about the view though. That's pretty spectacular."

"Alright, enough sightseeing, get to the bedroom already and see what's inside this safe," Blake ordered.

"You know you're quite bossy? Last time I checked you're essentially a bodyguard; you're not in charge of me."

"If you're too stupid to look after yourself then I will shanghai your decision-making skills," he said flatly.

"Ouch," I said. "Tell me how you really feel, Blake."

I made my way into the bedroom, a large four-poster bed draped in red silk dominating the space. "It smells like bachelor in here…" I murmured to myself.

"I'm a bachelor. What's that supposed to mean?" Blake asked.

"I'm choosing to not answer that question. Okay, if I was a safe where I would be? Jerry didn't exactly give me any clues." I checked the wardrobes and under the bed, but there was no sign of a safe. "Any ideas?" I asked Blake, pressing my finger against the earpiece.

"What's the floor like?"

"Carpet, square pattern," I said.

"It's probably hidden in a compartment under the floor. Stomp around a bit and see if you can hear a difference."

"Well, that shouldn't be too hard," I said, walking around like normal. Thanks to the spell heightening the amount of sound I made it sounded like I was stomping. I paced back and forth across the room until I heard a slight difference in the corner. Getting down on my hands and knees I found an invisible seam in the carpet and a square section lifted up from the floor. Underneath was the safe and combination pad. "Bingo!" I said. "Got it!"

"Hang on," Blake said. "There's a police car coming down the street, sirens blaring. It's overwhelming my senses. I'm finding it hard to hear you."

"I'm in the safe," I repeated, punching in the code that Jerry had given me. Sure enough the safe popped open. I pulled back the door and inside there was only one item—a small brown jar with a dropper cap. I picked up the jar and looked at it. "Huh. What the heck is this?"

Just then I felt the invisibility spell end. All of a sudden I could see my hands and body again.

"Zora, Zora!" Blake repeated. "The police are getting out in front of the building. Three cars just came out of nowhere. The police, they're running inside!"

"Wait, what?" I said, jumping to my feet. My heart started beating in my chest. My first instinct was that maybe something had happened to the guard, but then the truth of the matter hit me. "That son of a gun set me up!" I gasped.

"Zora, you have to get out of there now! It's a setup!" Blake shouted. "I can't hear anything you're saying, the sirens are too loud!"

"Dude, it's too late for me to get out! It'll take me like three minutes to recast the invisibility spell… maybe if I hustle really fast I can—" It was then that I heard the door to Mark Mobson's apartment crash open. The only thing I could think to do was hide my wand and the magical book. I hid them inside my aura where humans wouldn't be able to see them.

"Police! Come out with your hands up!"

I immediately started panicking; I'd never been in trouble before. What was I supposed to do? I did the only thing I could think of. I threw my hands in the air and started shouting over and over again. "I'm not armed! I'm not armed!"

"In the bedroom!" another voice came. Suddenly several flashlights were pointing in my direction, blinding me. "On your knees now, hands behind your back, fingers laced together!"

"I'm just trying to help!" I shouted, following their orders as they ran behind me and cuffed me. "This is not what it looks like! It's a setup!"

I don't know what was going to happen next, but one thing was clear. I'd messed up.

Big time.

* * *

SHERIFF BURT COMBS stared at me in disbelief from behind the shiny metal table in interview room one. "You know for an innocent lady you're remarkably good at looking guilty."

"And I can bake. How am I still single?" I said sarcastically.

"Wick, I think we're past the point of joking around," Burt said, looking reluctant to even have the conversation. "You know how bad this looks, right? I mean the first time wasn't great, but this… it don't exactly look like you're innocent. Breaking into the apartment of the person you killed—"

"Allegedly killed," I corrected.

"Allegedly killed… and all for what? To steal something from his safe? What was even in that little brown jar?"

"I don't know! Burt, you have to believe me. Jerry Mobson told me to go to that apartment. He said there's evidence that would help clear my name!"

Burt blinked. "Let me get this straight. Jerry Mobson—the superstar professional athlete—came to visit the woman accused of murdering his brother so he could help exonerate her?"

"When you put it that way it obviously seems crazy." I paused for a moment in self-reflection, wondering how I didn't see this setup coming. "Don't you think this stinks of a setup? How did the police know I was going to be there? Who even were those guys?! I thought this police station was a mom-and-pop operation!"

"They're from Eureka. They've got a SWAT unit over there. How they got there so fast and what they were doing in Compass Cove I don't know."

"They were tipped off!" I shouted again. "Obviously!"

"By Jerry Mobson," Burt reiterated. "The superstar athlete."

"Jerry came to me in the street. I talked to him!"

"Okay. Do you have proof of this conversation?" Burt asked.

"I… don't," I said, sinking slightly with defeat as I realized I was looking crazier by the minute. There was a knock on the door. Burt hollered a 'Yeah?' and his wife, Linda, opened it.

"I got Hannity on the line. Says he wants to talk to you."

"Honey on a hotdog," Burt said, rolling his eyes. "I better take it. You hold tight, Wick. You ain't going anywhere tonight." Burt shuffled out of the room, Linda sliding in to watch me.

"Suggestive implication," she said. "Eight letters."

"Seriously?" I said, looking at her. "Don't I even get a 'hello' now?"

"Hello, Zora Wick," Linda said without bothering to look up. "Eight letters, suggestive implication."

"Come on, this one is easy. You don't know this?"

Linda did look up at me now, her eyes fixed in a hard glare. "I enjoy crosswords. Never said I was good at them."

"Innuendo," I sighed.

A huge smile came over her face as she filled in the crossword. "I love you, Wick!" Linda tucked the book away and frowned at me. "Girl, if I have to say one thing about you… you're darned good at finding trouble. What's going on, Wick?"

"Short answer? I'm an idiot. Fell for a classic setup. I almost deserve the jail time."

"Well I know one thing for sure; you ain't getting out on bail, not tonight."

"I'm spending the night inside?!" I gasped.

Linda opened her eyes as though it was obvious. "Uh yeah, Wick? Come on. You're smarter than that. I'll make sure you get the comfortable cell though!"

"And here I thought my crossword skills would never pay off," I muttered.

The 'comfortable cell', as it turned out, was a regular jail cell with a hard concrete bench. The 'comfort' part was a scratchy gray blanket that smelled like old shoes. I lay there for hours, staring up at the ceiling when someone cleared their throat outside the bars. Looking up I saw Blake and Hudson.

"I'm either hallucinating or you two are standing there without fighting each other," I said.

"Blake filled me in on the night's events. I'll be honest. I'm a little mad he even let you go through with the plan, but you're very persuasive—I don't think I can fault him on this one," Hudson admitted.

"And you weren't there," Blake pointed out. "A bad guardian is better than an absent one."

Hudson glared at Blake, looking like he wanted to punch his lights out. Even if he did, he looked like he agreed with him, not that he'd say it out loud. "I had emergency MAGE business to attend to, and I've got more to see to now. I've got to split out of town for a day. Timing is horrible, but it is what it is. I'm putting you in Blake's hands."

Blake nodded. "You're my problem now, and let's be honest—a jail cell is probably the safest place for you to be. I don't have to worry about you slipping out of my fingers."

"This is what it takes for you both to get along?" I asked. "Seeing me locked up?"

"Makes our lives a lot easier," Hudson commented. "You're very good at running around and finding trouble. Blake is right. At least now you're confined to this concrete room."

"Ugh," I sighed. "I hate my life."

Hudson's watch started flashing. He looked at it and dismissed the notification. "I've got to go." He eyed Blake and then me. "Stay safe, Zora. We'll sort this out when I get back."

"Yeah, yeah," I muttered. Hudson left, leaving Blake outside the cell. "What is it?" I asked.

"We're going to fix this," he said. "I promise. You want to talk?"

"No, I just want to be left alone."

Blake held up his hands. "Say no more. I'll come and check on you in an hour."

Once Blake was gone, I rolled over to try and get some sleep, screaming as I saw the ghostly face of my Aunt Constance sticking through the wall. I scrambled backwards off the bed and landed on the cold hard floor.

"Constance!" I yelled.

"Sorry," she said. "I wanted to check in on my favorite niece and see how she's doing."

"As you can see, things are going really well for me," I said, gesturing to the jail cell. Constance had a huge grin on her face still. "Why... why are you looking at me like that?"

"I brought you something!" she said delightedly. "Aunt Constance has found a way for you to get out of this mess!"

"Go on then," I said, waiting for her to elaborate.

Constance floated through the wall properly, bringing another ghost with her.

It was Mark Mobson.

CHAPTER 21

"**You**!" I gasped.

"Yeah, me, big deal, get over it," Mark said flippantly.

"I caught this guy down at the gym spying in the women's locker rooms! What a degenerate!" Constance said.

I stared at her. "Don't you do the same thing, but with the guys?"

"That's different!" Constance said. "Anyway, ol' mothball Mark here has something to tell you."

"Can you stop calling me that?" Mark sighed, rolling his eyes. "It doesn't make any sense!"

"Let's speed this along, yeah?" I said to the arguing ghosts. "I don't know if you guys are aware, but things aren't exactly going well for me here."

"Oh, I'm sorry, little miss 'I'm still alive'!" Mark said sarcastically. "I guess I'll just take my information and get out of here!" Mark went to float out of the cell when I jumped to my feet.

"No! Wait. Wait! I'm sorry. Please, just tell me what you know."

Mark considered it and turned around in the air to face me again. "I want you to admit something to me first."

"What?" I asked.

"Admit you were attracted to me," he said, folding his arms over his chest.

I looked at Constance in despair and then back at Mark. In my most deadpan delivery I parroted the words back to him. "I was attracted to you."

"I knew it!" Mark said, punching the air and flying around in loops. He looked at Constance and jabbed his finger. "I told you! All the women dig Mark Mobson."

"Yes, you're quite the catch, like gonorrhea or chlamydia," Constance said sarcastically.

"Spill the beans, ghost boy, I'm getting bored," I said.

"I take it you already know who killed me?" he asked.

"I don't have anything concrete, but my intuition is leaning towards your brother," I said.

"Yeah, can you believe that? That scumbag!" Mark shouted. "What did I do to deserve that?!"

"You seriously don't know?" I said in disbelief. Mark threw his hands in the air as if he didn't.

"Please, enlighten me!"

"You know that he killed you, but not why?" I asked.

"I've been following him around town since I became a ghost," Mark said. "He's got all the evidence!"

"Dude, you basically bankrupted your brother," I said. "He's clearly struggling financially, trying to support his entire extended family and sinking cash into your money pit of a club."

"Hey, the club is going to turn around any day now!" Mark said, still suffering from the delusion that he was a great businessman.

"Sure," I said. "Listen, you said he had evidence. What do you know?"

"Oh yeah, it's all in this warehouse on Baluga Avenue! A jar of white chocolate drops, the poison—which he planted in the safe at my apartment to frame you! He even got the recipe for the brownies from my ex-wife, that snake! Jerry's great friends with the police over in Eureka; they love him. I bet he called ahead of time to get that sting set up."

"I'm guessing he saw your stream, knew you had the brownie in your pocket, and switched it out at some point. Did you see your brother that day?"

"Yeah, I met him for lunch, it was his idea! Though I don't know when he could have switched the brownie out—actually, I *did* go to the bathroom at one point to try and hit on this chick."

"Okay, all I have to do is give the police the address for this place and this nightmare can be over!" I said.

"You'd better hurry though," Mark said. "Last I saw he was torching everything."

I froze. "Wait, what?"

"Yeah, he's got a big metal barrel and some kerosene. I mean he hasn't started the fire yet, but it's obviously going to go up like Fourth of July."

I looked at Constance with some alarm. "I have to get over there now and stop that guy!"

"Uh, call the police?" she suggested.

I shook my head. "No, they won't move fast enough, and Blake won't let me handle this. How do I get out of this cell, quickly?"

"You want an intangibility spell. Ooh, bonus! If you're intangible, then I can hold your hand and fly you over to this place!"

"Intangible?" I asked.

"Basically, means you can walk through walls. You become a ghost!"

I pulled the magic book out of my aura and flicked through until I found a spell for intangibility.

Intangibility.

The ability to pass through walls and other solid objects for at least one minute!

"Uh, I'm loathe to use this book again, but I don't really have any other options."

Constance smirked. "Aga Bizva? His spells are always so hokey!"

"Yeah, I'm not exactly swimming with choice." I pulled my wand out and quickly worked through the spell. As it activated a footnote appeared on the page.

Footnote: After this spell all other magic will be amplified by a factor of ten for twenty-four hours.

"You hack!" I shouted at the book's author, stashing it back in my magical aura. Without warning Constance grabbed my hand and smiled at me.

"Ready to go on a little ride?!" she sang. We rushed up through the ceiling of the police station and high into the sky over Compass Cove.

We arrived at the old warehouse just as the spell ended and I landed on the sidewalk. "You smell that?" I shouted to Constance. "Burning!"

"No sense of smell as a ghost, but I trust you!" She popped her head through the corrugated door in front of us and popped it out again. "It's him, he's around the back, he's got a flaming oil barrel! He's about to burn the evidence!"

I started sprinting down an alley that led to the back of the warehouse. As I skidded around the corner I saw Jerry Mobson standing next to the barrel, his hands held over the flames. A small wooden box was next to him on a chair, no doubt the evidence he was about to burn. His eyes lit up upon seeing me.

"You?!" he said. "But, how?!"

"Never mind that!" I shouted back. "You're not burning that evidence!"

I don't know exactly what I was planning, but I started running towards Jerry, perhaps imagining that he was going to run away from me—that's what criminals always did in the crime shows. Instead, he waited until I was about ten feet away and then he charged *at* me.

"Hey, wait, no! You're supposed to run!" I screamed, trying to turn and sprint away as he reached out for me. I was too late. Jerry seized me in a bear hug and carried me into the warehouse.

"Is that so?" he laughed. "I spent my entire life running, chasing that damn ball, marching to the beat of my family's drum. I ain't running no longer. I'm sick of it!"

"Help!" I screamed. "Help! Help!"

"Oh shut up," Jerry said. He held me under one arm like I weighed nothing at all, my arms crushed against my sides so I couldn't do anything. With his free hand he punched a red button on the wall, closing the warehouse's rear door. "No one will hear you around here anyway, not at this time of night."

Jerry marched me over to an old chair in the middle of the derelict warehouse and strapped me to it using duct tape. I tried to fight him, but he was just too strong.

"Use your magic!" Constance bellowed all the while.

"I haven't got any left!" I growled back. Jerry shot me a confused look.

"Who the heck are you talking to?" he asked.

"Doesn't matter," I said. "You're not going to get away with this!"

"I already got away with killing my freeloader of a brother. What makes you so different?" he asked, pulling a small glass bottle out of his pocket. Strychnine.

"Where are you getting this stuff?" I asked.

"Rats," he said. "I've got rats at my house. Got the exterminator in, but the rats are still there. I stole a couple of vials of this stuff from the back of his van when he wasn't looking."

I looked down at Jerry's sneakers, still covered in tiny holes. "That explains why your shoes are so beat up," I said. At first I thought a small dog had been at them.

"I've got no money left, Miss Wick. It's gone. All gone! Can't even afford to replace my shoes! Mark had to go, he was too much of a liability. I loved my brother, but he bankrupted me."

"You could have just said no," I pointed out.

"No. I'm the strong one, I'm the champion. I don't let my family down. I provide, like a real man."

"Does a real man kill his own brother because he's too afraid to admit that he's broke? It's okay to fail, dude."

"I'm not a failure!" Jerry screamed; the resulting silence was deafening. "Anyway, no need to drag this out any longer than necessary. You can take the strychnine too and I'll burn your body with the rest of the evidence. Once that's taken care of this mess is done."

Jerry pulled the top off the bottle of poison and grabbed my jaw with other hand.

"You don't need to do this!" I said. "You're making a big mistake!" I had no magic left and death was seconds away. I had to think of something.

"Sorry, Miss Wick, it's nothing personal," he said. Jerry went to pour the bottle into my mouth when a last-minute idea came to me. I needed a spell that didn't require any magic.

"Phone book!" I screamed.

Jerry paused, and for a second nothing happened, but then a dozen portals opened up behind him and multiple copies of the magical phone book flew forward and smashed into the football player. The final book caught him on the side of the head and he dropped to the ground, unconscious.

Constance just stared in amazement. "I've never seen that many come at once!"

"Thank the lord for side effects from crappy spells," I said with a sigh of relief. Just then a portal opened in front of me, and Hudson dropped out.

"Zora!" he began.

"Ah, your magical defense system worked just in the nick of time, Hudson," I said sarcastically.

"Are you okay?!" he gasped.

"I'm fine. Get me out of this chair. I've got the killer and the evidence is safe outside."

The mystery was done.

CHAPTER 22

"*A*ll yours!" Bitz said, handing the keys back to me. "I'm proud to announce that your apartment and business are completely Poxy free!"

"Thank you, thank you, *thank you*," I said sincerely, smiling at Bitz and closing the door behind him. I walked into my apartment and let out a big sigh of relief, smelling in the familiar scent of home.

"Well, I'm going to hit the hay," Hermes said, jogging past me towards his cat bad. "What a crazy week for me!"

I rolled my eyes. "Yeah, I'm sure the last few days have been really challenging for you." I walked into the living room and stopped at Phoebe's cage. The owl opened her eyes slowly and yawned.

"It's going to rain tomorrow," she said.

"It always rains here," I said with a chuckle. "Listen, no offense, but I'm starting to think Hermes is onto something here. It's okay if you just tell the weather and the time; you don't have to pretend you can do anything more than that." Though upon reflection I *had* seen Phoebe do some pretty weird things when she was tired.

Phoebe blinked slowly again. "I have more powers, but I'm limited to what I can show you; your powers are still relatively small. Once your abilities grow, I can show you more of my capabilities."

"Sure thing, Phoebe," I said, giving her a playful scritch on the side of the head. Just then the doorbell rang. I went over to the buzzer. "Yup?" I asked.

"It's Blake. You got a minute?"

I went down the stairs and opened the door to see him standing there with a bouquet of flowers.

"What's this?" I said in amazement.

"I wanted to congratulate you on officially reopening the bakery. I know it's been a tough week for you, and I just wanted you to know that I've always got your back."

"Thanks," I said, feeling myself blush as I took the flowers. "Do you want to come in for a drink?"

Blake raised a suggestive brow.

"It's just a drink," I reiterated. "Don't get ahead of yourself, wolf boy."

He laughed. "I'm just kidding. I've actually got to head back to the station and take care of something for Burt, but let's take a rain check on that drink. Maybe it could be a drink and a dinner sometime?"

"That sounds a lot like a date..." I said.

Blake shrugged. "Hey, your words, not mine. Stay safe, Zora Wick."

With that Blake jumped out of sight. I closed the door, headed back upstairs, and put the flowers in the kitchen. The doorbell rang again.

"Sheesh, I'm never gonna get a nap in at this rate," I said to myself. I went over to the buzzer and pressed it. "Hello?"

"Hey, it's Hudson. You got a minute?"

I laughed to myself and went downstairs. Upon opening the door, I saw Hudson standing there with an identical bouquet of flowers. I smiled at him in a puzzled manner and took the flowers.

"What?" he asked.

"You didn't just see who was here?" I asked.

"No," he said and shook his head. "Are you in trouble?"

"No, it's nothing; don't worry about it. The flowers are lovely. To what do I owe the pleasure?"

"Just congratulating you on surviving another week in Compass Cove."

I smiled. "Thanks. You want a drink?"

"I'd love to, but I've got MAGE things to take care of. Another time?"

I laughed again and nodded my head. "Sure. See you around, Hudson."

"See you around, Zora Wick," Hudson said, winking as he slipped out of sight.

Once again I closed the door and made my way upstairs, putting Hudson's flowers next to Blake's. I made my way into the living room, searching for something to do.

"Where's Zelda?" I muttered to myself. "Maybe she wants to hang out."

"Fine," Phoebe blurted. I looked at her.

"Huh?"

"I'll reveal another one of my abilities. I think you've earned it. You might not be all-powerful, but I think you've proven you're a very capable witch. Ask me where Zelda is."

"Uh... okay. Where is Zelda?"

Phoebe's eyes went white, and she gave the answer in a robotic-like voice. "Zelda is in Compass Cove, two miles west."

"Woah!" I said. "What was that?!"

"I can tell you the location of people close to you," Phoebe said. "At all times. I think you've earned it."

"Huh. Let's try another. Where's... Sabrina?"

Again her eyes went white. "Sabrina is in Compass Cove, one mile north-east."

Like a child I started playing with the feature, rattling through the names of everyone I knew. Blake. *Compass Cove Police Station.* Hudson. *MAGE HQ – Location unknown.* Celeste. *Compass Cove docks.*

"Well, that sure is neat... thanks, Phoebe." I turned away from the time owl when an idea suddenly came to me. I looked back at her again and gave another name. "Hey, Phoebe... where is my mother?"

Phoebe's eyes went white but this time she didn't answer straight away. After a few seconds she spoke. "Compass Cove. This apartment. In the bathroom."

My heart started pounding in my chest, I stared at the owl for a moment, wondering if she'd really just said those words. I turned on my heels and ran to the bathroom, hammering the light switch only to find an empty room.

Then I noticed something. A reflection was standing in the mirror, a woman I had only ever seen in photographs before. She saw me, opened her eyes wide, and bolted out of the mirror.

It was my mother.

THANKS FOR READING

Thanks for reading, I hope you enjoyed the book.

It would really help me out if you could leave an honest review with your thoughts and rating on Amazon.

Every bit of feedback helps!

OTHER SERIES BY MARA WEBB

~ Ongoing ~

Compass Cove Cozy Mysteries

Midlife Strikes

An English Enchantment

~ Completed ~

Wicked Witches of Pendle Island

Hallow Haven Witch Mysteries

Wildes Witches Mysteries

Raven Bay Mysteries

Wicked Witches of Vanish Valley

MAILING LIST

Want to be notified when I release my latest book? Join my mailing list. It's for new releases only. No spam:

Click here to join!

I'll also send you a free 120,000 word book as a thank you for signing up.

marawebbauthor.com

amazon.com/-/e/B081X754NL
facebook.com/marawebbauthor
twitter.com/marawebbauthor
bookbub.com/authors/mara-webb

Printed in Great Britain
by Amazon

38509319R00111